GH01033725

Gabriel's Gate

A Book Republic Production

Published in 2011 by Book Republic, A division of Maverick House Publishers.

Office 19, Dunboyne Business Park, Dunboyne, Co. Meath, Ireland.

http://www.bookrepublic.ie
info@bookrepublic.ie

ISBN: 9781907221316

Text copyright © 2011 Tom Galvin

Internal layout © 2011 Book Republic

10 9 8 7 6 5 4 3 2 1

The paper used in this book comes from wood pulp of managed forests. For every tree felled, at least one tree is planted, thereby renewing natural resources.

A CIP catalogue record for this book is available form the British Library and the Irish Copyright libraries.

GABRIEL'S GATE

TOM GALVIN

BOOK REPUBLIC

A BOUTIQUE PUBLISHING PRESS

For Asia, Alex and Alicia; three angels

One

In an empty schoolyard, crows swooped down from the branches of trees and pulled at the remains of food scattered on the concrete floor. Bread crusts were torn apart with their beaks, empty crisp bags ripped asunder. Dozens of large black crows.

G watched them through the window, his thumb and forefinger meeting to form a small circle through which he could view a single crow at random. He imagined it was the sight on a rifle and that before the bell rang he was going to shoot them all. Crows, his grandmother had told him, came from hell. They were the devil's eyes during the day because the devil could only come out at night. All the other birds were sent by God, Jesus and the angels.

It was a long afternoon, the school was less than a week away from the Christmas holidays and the kids were all restless. One kid, a big guy nicknamed Spud, was starting to hassle this other kid up at the front called Green, a small, thin kid who was among the quieter ones in the class. Spud was beginning to get at Green, passing him notes about how he was going to come and get his sister. And he might even go after his mother. Green was trying his best to ignore it, but the notes were coming faster and the threats getting stronger and all the time G, who sat behind Green, was looking at the notes over his shoulder.

Now Spud was a real bully. A great big guy who wore hard boots and always had an improvised weapon of some kind close to hand. A ruler, a stick, a rope with a large knot in it – which was his favourite – or sometimes he had a knife. But nobody had ever seen him actually use the knife on anyone. He just scratched his initials on the desks with it. But he was one of these guys who turned school into hell and had started robbing money and lunches a few months earlier with a small gang of his, threatening to beat up other kids if they didn't hand over the goods. The only ones to get away with it were the girls, simply because he was afraid of them.

So within a few minutes Green started to become scared, shifting around in his chair and looking up at the teacher, who was too old and had little control over the class and was oblivious to the goings on. Finally G turned around and told Spud to leave it alone. Spud just drew a finger across his throat and pointed two fingers back at G, before leaning over the desk and slapping him on the ear.

Bell went, teacher left. Suddenly Spud walked over to Green and gave him a dig in the gut that knocked him out of his desk and onto the floor. It was a rabbit punch, fast and sharp, beneath the ribs. Poor guy hit the floor like a plank and within seconds a pool of piss began forming on the tiled floor, right there in front of the class, girls and all. Spud got a great kick out of this, him and his mates watching Green lying there, the whole class laughing.

Then out of nowhere there came a scream so unexpected that the laughing ceased like it had just been swallowed up. It came again, louder even than the crows that cawed and scraped outside in the yard. People turned to see Spud, a look of terror on his face, leaning back against the wall. Then he fell, down onto the floor next to Green.

The class had gone from laughter to startled silence and in the centre of the room stood G with a large blackboard compass in his hand. He dropped it when he realised what he had done, but it was too late. One girl screamed, followed by another, and within minutes the duty teacher on the corridor rushed in.

G was forced to wait until after the school had emptied of children. He waited a full two hours, sitting outside the headmaster's office in the deathly quiet corridor with the yellow lights humming above his head, waiting until a report came back from the hospital. He had all that time to dwell on what he had done — driven the blackboard compass into Spud's thigh. He savoured the image, the comical side of it at least, knowing that he was in deep trouble once the headmaster called him in.

He would probably be expelled.

'I think you're a lucky young lad. Have you anything to say for yourself?'

G looked at the headmaster, then over to the clock on the wall. It was after 6.00pm. Three hours he had been waiting.

'So, you've nothing to say? Nothing at all? You know what you could have done. Or did you even think about it? He could have bled to death in minutes.'

The headmaster moved closer to G and sat down. He stared hard at him for a full minute then finally put his hand under the boy's chin and lifted his head.

'Why did you do it?'

'I don't know, Sir.'

'You do know. Why did you do it?'

'I don't know.'

The headmaster let go of G's chin and stood up and walked over to the window as dusk turned over and the street lights blinked a couple of times then shone yellow. He was a fair man and had been through tough times in tough schools in the inner and the outer city and had seen every type come and go. He knew well how to handle these kids.

He moved back to the desk, rearranged G's file and scanned it again, the grades, remarks and the potential all right there in his hands.

'I'm going to be watching you carefully. And you're going to be reporting to me every Friday for an hour's detention. That will be reviewed at the end of next term. I could have thrown you out, you know that.'

G glanced up quickly.

'Have you got a problem with that?'

'No, Sir.'

'All right. Now go on home.'

G turned as he reached the door and looked up at the headmaster.

'Sir?'

'What is it?'

'Somebody had to do something, didn't they? I mean, it isn't fair.'

The headmaster closed the file and pushed it to one side of his desk.

'No, you're right, it's not fair. But you just have to know when to act and when to leave things as they are and let others take charge. You'll learn that someday. Now off you go. It's getting late.'

G left the school as fingers of darkness crept in across the sky. In the yard, a few remaining crows screeched and G stood and watched them until the sky grew too dark and the birds became invisible against its great black curtain. He ran through the gate to the shelter of the streetlamps which were casting a glow on the pavements that crackled with fallen leaves. Soon the crows would disappear. Off to wherever it was they went when night fell. And then he would be home.

Two

Out in a distant field, a dark shadow descended on the cold damp muck; crows, hundreds of them. They came down from the sky where they had waited like a rain cloud, circling until the tractor had gone.

G watched them as they pecked at the ground and gouged the freshly ploughed earth asunder until it seemed there could be nothing left alive in there, not even one solitary worm.

He turned towards the forest, beyond a paddock where a few glasshouses stood, full of withering tomato plants choked by weeds. A river curled its way into the forest before dipping out of sight. Beyond that, fields and more fields, rolling into one another, up and over as far as the eye could see.

On his left was the farmhouse. In front, a fine garden at the end of a laneway with a natural arch formed by branches from the trees either side, some older than him by three, four, five generations, with huge boughs you could hide in for days. Next to him was the barnyard, the moss on the concrete was the colour of emeralds, and a corrugated iron roof scorched by the sun and ravaged by rain was rinsed to the colour of ochre. There was a stable and other outhouses, and everywhere there lay tyres and machinery parts, boxes and empty cloth sacks, crates and baskets, cages and rolls of chicken wire.

A gravel path led from where he stood, up towards the front of the house through a small green gate in a low stone wall that separated the rest of the farm from the house and gardens.

G heard the gravel crunch behind him and turned to see John coming down the path with a bottle in each hand, brown with no labels and metal hoops at the top. He handed one to G.

'Homemade cider. Made with our own apples.'

G grabbed the cool glass bottle and put it to his lips. As he tilted it back the sun hit him in the eyes and the taste of sour apples hit the back of his throat.

'So what do you think of the place?'

G took another swig of the cider and looked about.

'I think it's going to be perfect. Perfect John, just like this stuff here.'

He belched then spat a string at a coil of chicken wire with a cobweb at the centre.

'Perfect.'

They walked back up the path and through the gate towards the main house, swinging their bottles by the steel hoops and kicking at weeds that poked through the gravel. The front door was a heavy solid piece of work that swung open into a long hall full of old furniture covered with sheets. The floorboards were thick and stained dark, a faint smell of damp rising from beneath them. There were three rooms to the left, one straight ahead at the end, and on the right stood the large staircase, one arm leading up, another leading down into the kitchen.

G took a few steps forward and poked his head into the first room which smelled of burned logs that came from a pile of ash sitting in the mouth of a large fireplace, a huge cast iron grate decorated with the head of a fox at either end.

'Needs a bit of work, G.'

'I know it does. When was the last time this was used by anyone?'

John shrugged and kept his arms folded across his chest.

'Months. Many months. Why?'

'The ashes are still in the hearth.'

'That's 'cos there was a fire there. What did you expect?'

G kicked the ashes with his boot; it was like kicking plaster.

'That they'd be cleaned out.'

'They're cleaned out when you go to light the next fire, G. Jesus.'

G nodded.

'It's perfect, John.'

G left the room and walked down the hall with John following. He pushed the next door which opened into a smaller room, a dining room with an old wooden table and high-backed chairs with patterned wine and white upholstery.

'This can be the office.'

'Office?'

'Office, John. We need some sort of order. We'll have it all worked out. Everyone will have a job, a function. Just like a monastery. And we need to be on top of finances.'

He glanced at John.

'Sure.'

'How many bedrooms have we got? In total.'

'Six. Two with bathrooms, but they all have sinks. There's a large bathroom at the end of the corridor. We can convert the small room at the end here into a larger bathroom as well if we want it. There's a guest toilet down the stairs next to the kitchen. It all needs a bit of elbow grease G, really. There's been no one in this place now for months. It has to be painted. We need to sand all the wooden floors. A lot of work.'

'Nine… how many will we fit in at the start?'

'Ten or twelve anyway.'

'Twelve. What about outside, any good?'

'Could be. There's the few old sheds and the workers' rooms.'

'The workers' rooms, what are they?'

'The outhouses you saw near the barn. In the good old days, the uncle had a few farmhands that stayed there during the week. But I wouldn't put a dog in them now, G.'

'How many, John? Forget the condition.'

'You'd be talking four or five. Max.'

'Four or five. We'll try and get someone down here as soon as possible. Get hold of someone with building experience. Go over the whole place and get a quote on costs and time.'

'There's only five of us at the minute. That's if you convince your pals.'

'They'll come, John. Don't you worry about it.'

'Build it and they will come, sort of thing.'

'They always do.'

G sat on the second step of the stairs and stared up at the ceiling, high with a decorated border and a chandelier hanging from its centre. He could hear the voices already. The laughter, the music, the singing. The smells from the kitchen in the evening and the cold wet muck from the fields.

'What the hell was your uncle doing with such a big place, John?'

'It's old, G. He came from a big family who all lived here for generations. He had a small family though, that was his mistake. Actually only a son and a daughter, which was why the place went to hell. It was too big, and the first chance the son got he was gone to the States. The daughter went to London. Both of them left in the eighties in the last recession. Off they went.'

'Would you blame them?'

'Yeah. I would. It left me uncle short, didn't it?'

'Which is where you came in.'

'Yeah. And I was only a kid. A boy. But I worked here every year during the summer when I was in school. Picking spuds, working in the glasshouses in the heat. Whatever I could do. Loved it. Even in college, G, I'd be back some weekends to help out. Until this year of course, when he died and the place was left.' His face saddened at the thought.

'So why did you hang on to it?'

'Land, G. It's something I wouldn't expect you to

understand with the way things have been going the last few years. But you never give up land, and if it's in the family, you keep it there. And as soon as the uncle died the son and daughter were back scratching around for their inheritance. But of course they discovered the place was worth nothing. It used to be. But not anymore. Plus there were the debts. So they just headed away again.'

'And you stayed.'

'You never leave your roots for too long, G. If you cut something off from its roots it's as good as dead.'

The grandfather clock in the hallway chimed three times.

'Do you want to look upstairs?'

G walked from one room to the next, lifting sheets from bits of furniture, peering under beds and poking his head into wardrobes, while John sat humming to himself on the large landing at the end of the corridor atop an old couch which was busting at the sides.

'Well? Which room do you want tonight?'

'Are there any decent beds?'

'Don't worry, you won't die in them. You can grab a duvet from the hot press here, they'll be all right.'

G looked at the press beside the old couch John was sitting on. He stared at John, fidgeting with the bits and pieces he had in his pockets.

'Can't be very hot though, can it?'

'Freezing actually, but the sheets in it are clean. Now come on, you've seen enough for one day.'

They walked down the hill from the farm with John stopping at every bend to point things out in the distance or even up close, whatever took his fancy. And by the time they reached his favourite pub, which was at the far end of town, it was close to evening.

They stood at the bar on a cold stone floor, an empty fireplace at their backs which should have been ablaze. John sipped his pint and turned and put a hand out towards it.

'Thought the fire would be lit. Place used to be hopping.'

'It is only Wednesday. And it's only seven o'clock.'

'Doesn't matter. You'd always have people in here. Used to come here with my uncle. Sat right there in that far corner so we could see the musicians opposite. When I was a kid it was lemonade and crisps. Then when I was a bit older it was half lemonade and half ale and crisps. Then when I was old enough it was pints of this stuff.'

John raised his pint of stout and took a long swig leaving a coffee-coloured blob under his nose.

'Lot of memories belong in here, G. They're all ghosts now.'

'What happened to the crisps?'

'They got too expensive.'

They made the walk back up the hill and John lit the fire, having poked the ashes down under the grate then pushed them aside to allow a draught to sweep through. Soon the flames were licking the back of the flue and the foxes' heads shimmered. They got bottles of cider and pulled the tops open, drinking liberally while the wind outside shook the window panes.

'What problems are we going to have, John?'

John sighed loudly and rested his head back on the armchair.

'There will be problems, G. And there were a few things that I didn't bring up with you because they are things that you'll have to simply discover as you go along.'

'Like what? Give me an example.'

'Well, you don't have any experience of life on farms. And the type of thing we're going to be doing will be hard grafting, G. It will be tough. And it will get ugly. We'll have to do many things the old way, because, well, we don't have the money for all the equipment we need. I had to sell most of it off.'

'So, give me an example.'

'Well, there'll be handpicking potatoes, sewing crops, pulling up cabbages, planting, pruning, mucking out shit from sheds. Jesus. I could go on forever. But that's all just hard work. There are other things about life here, harsher, crueller things, G. Did you ever have to kill an animal? They have faces, you know.'

G turned and looked at John, unamused.

'I know they have faces, man. Jesus.'

'Well, you don't see a face on a steak. That's all I'm saying. But I've killed animals, we were licensed to do it for years. The uncle stopped as it became too cumbersome, but in the beginning I helped him out when it was small scale enough. You'll see things differently here, G. It's closer to nature and nature, you know, doesn't have compassion. Nature just does what it does. But it's probably time we got back to it. Do us all some good.'

Out in the hall the grandfather clock chimed twice as G crawled up into one of the empty rooms, tore off his boots and jeans and pulled a duvet over him. He felt at ease, despite the fact they were all alone in this huge place, acres of land all around them, all of it drenched in darkness: the fields and forests that swept across the countryside; the desolate buildings and deserted towns; the nocturnal animals out in the fields, crawling through the hedgerows, scampering on the floor of the woods; the wind blowing in gusts and the branches of trees tapping on the windows; the empty corridors and the floorboards that creaked all by themselves. G slept like the dead.

Three

G tore a lump from the grass and shook off the earth, staring at the colour of the roots, a sandy brown against the green at the tip.

Mack stared at him.

'What the hell are you doing?'

'Look at the colour of the roots. Brown. A reddish brown. How come they're brown when the grass is green?'

'Cos they're in the muck. Are we going or not?'

When G and a couple of his mates decided to run away, they never had any reason. 'Running away' was something they felt you should do. It was G's idea. He brought it up first and his mates didn't take much convincing, because, as G had worked out, even back then, people don't need a lot of convincing when it comes to a natural impulse. If he felt so strongly about doing something, then there would be others out there who felt the same. It was a very simple logic and it was how people became leaders. No matter how seemingly ridiculous an act is, there will always be someone wanting to follow.

It was with two friends that G ran away. Duff and Macker. Mack was a tough nut, but Duff was pretty soft. They were three good friends, in school at least. And when the day came to run away, they all met up as planned, down behind the football pitch where there was a bit of a wood and a stream with a swing over it made from a tyre that Macker had robbed from a garage.

It was a good swing, but the bootboys cut it down every so often and threw it in the river. G's ma had always called them the bootboys, and they were what his mates had warned him about when he'd left his first home. There hadn't been many bootboys there, at least not like these guys. Anyway, they weren't wearing boots anymore. Their clothes were changing too. They wore runners more than anything else, and hoodies too. But in G's eyes, they would still be called 'the bootboys' regardless of what they wore.

When all three met up behind the football pitch that day, they had to make a swear not to tell anyone. Duff had looked scared. He didn't want to make a swear, so Macker gave him a small slap on the head and asked him why.

Turned out that he'd already told his mother that morning that he was running away. Macker couldn't believe it. The whole idea of running away was that nobody knows you're doing it, he said. But Duff didn't understand what he'd done wrong. He always told his mother everything. G thought it was funny. Now the whole thing was ruined. G said it didn't matter. They could still go.

They got on the bus to the city centre. It was a Saturday and the town was packed full of shoppers and other kids like themselves. G liked going to town. He used to go with his sister before she left, and sometimes with her boyfriend. The boyfriend used to tell G about the days when he was a very young Mod. In those days, there were rockers, punks and skas, he said. And a lot of the time there were fights and he used to get stuck in. He told G that now people just scrapped with each other for no real reason at all and that at least when he was a kid he had something to fight for. G didn't like him. And G's da hated him and used to try and ground his sister on the weekend. But she always did what she wanted.

The plan was to go into town and find somewhere to hide. All three were dressed in combat gear they had bought in an army shop the previous summer. They thought it was the best thing to wear. But once they started walking around town they realised how stupid the whole idea was.

Macker had said he had money and they were going to buy more food and stuff. Turned out he'd no money at all. Himself and Duff went into a few shops and knocked off a pile of gear. Even stuff they didn't need.

They spent the afternoon walking around town and then went into the park to eat some of the food they'd brought with them, crackers, apples and some baby biscuits that Macker had nicked from his sister who'd had a kid a couple of months earlier. After they closed the park, they decided to go back to their camp. That was the best place.

When they got back it was getting dark and the football pitch was deserted, the reek of wet winter muck blowing over it on a cold wind. They had a load of cigarettes and boxes of matches and they lit a fire, deciding to stay there for the night. But it got colder and Duff wanted to go home. He was hungry and his ma always had a fry on Saturday for supper.

G's ma would have a fry as well. The smell of it always hung in the garden on Saturday evenings, mixed with the coal from the fire she lit on weekends. Duff wanted to know why they were running away anyway. G just told him that everybody does it sometime. It's what you do. Macker agreed with him.

About 7.00pm, Duff's mother came across the pitch looking for him. Duff just stood up and went. Just like that. He didn't even try and hide or anything. He heard her calling him and he said goodnight to the lads and left. They could hear her in the field telling him his tea was ready and her asking him where the hell he'd been all day. Then there was the sound of an ear being slapped but they didn't hear Duff cry.

G and Macker stayed a while longer until they heard the bootboys coming in the distance. There was a sort of unspoken rule that if you're only a kid, you left the football pitch after dark. If you were still around when the bootboys came, you were dead.

They were older, most of them, and had cans and drugs with them, and sometimes girls. That worked out better if you were caught because the girls would usually feel sorry for you and tell the bootboys to let you go.

When G heard the bootboys coming he wanted to run. He felt it in his gut, his heart pounding and the blood in his ears. He hated the bootboys and often dreamed of getting them. Sometimes he'd have nightmares where they'd get him instead and this would make his hatred grow. He'd lie awake some nights listening to them on the street outside shouting and he'd imagine one of them getting hit by a car. Any one of them, it didn't matter. The way he saw it, one less of them meant one less to watch out for when he was walking home in the evenings, because one of them had kicked him in the head when he was coming back from the shop once.

He had only been in the new housing estate about a month and his ma had sent him down to the local stores to get stuff for supper. He was walking down the path when he saw two of them coming towards him. One of them was a good few yards ahead of the other and just as he passed G, he turned to his mate and told him to kick G in the head. G thought he was joking. There was no reason to do it, anyway G was half their size. But he did it anyway. As he walked past G, he lifted his leg and kicked G in the head. G went dizzy for a second and fell on the path. It didn't hurt so much, and G was thankful that they had started wearing runners. But G's money and the thing he had bought for supper flew out of his hand, including eggs; G heard them crack. The bootboys just thought it was funny. He lay there on the ground for a minute because there was nobody around to help him.

It was just like Green when Spud and the lads had eventually got him. Green had been a good companion in school. But he grew too soft and began to depend on G after what he had done for him a couple of years earlier. Finally, one day G dropped him. There was nothing else for it. And anyway, G had become better mates with Macker and Duff.

G remembered the day well. He knew Green was in trouble. He saw it coming a mile away, but Green didn't. He'd no instinct, he was too naive and left everything up to G. On this particular day, Spud and the lads were out to get Green because they knew G had begun to abandon him. Nobody messed with G in school after they heard what he had done to Spud. And Spud had never forgotten that Green had sung like a bird while he was in hospital and Spud was the type of guy that would carry the weight of vengeance around with him for years.

When school ended that day, Green went up to the woodwork room where G had his last lesson. They had nearly always gone home together but those days were becoming few and far between and this was one of the days G had stalled. He told Green he had to stay back to do the sweeping up because it was his turn on the cleaning rota and poor Green looked nervous. He never liked to go home alone but he was usually safe with G. G couldn't look him in the eye. Green finally left and G watched him go out through the school gates. He walked out slowly, and as he went through the gate he turned and waved at G. But G didn't wave back. He kept sweeping the floor and waited half an hour for the next bus.

Green never forgave him. He didn't come in the next day, or the day after that, and when he did he was bruised and battered after the guys had kicked the hell out of him, dragging him across the football pitch and into the trees behind it for a good beating. G felt sorry for him when he saw him, he could have been there and done something.

They didn't talk after that. For a while G thought he really had done the right thing. He thought that Green was better off learning the hard way that things just weren't fair. That G wouldn't be around forever. But things just went from bad to worse as the guys went after Green more, knowing he was an easy target. Some evenings G would walk down the road after getting off the bus and hear the screams in the distance. Sometimes Green would call him, his voice screaming across the football pitch, cold and deserted in the windy winter evenings. But G never went back to help. Within a few months Green was taken out of the school and G never saw him again.

There are times when a good friend will walk away. G's da had told him that when he was small. Not because he wants to, but because good friends know they won't always be there. Nobody can always be there.

So when G heard the bootboys coming he wanted to go. Macker didn't. He told G that you can never let people scare you like that, stop you doing what you want to do. But Macker was older than G and he had brothers. G's sister loved him but she was never any good with the bootboys. So G decided he'd go. He stood and moved into the trees and watched the bootboys move closer.

There were at least eight of them and one of them had a knife. Finally, G went back and grabbed Macker, telling him he had to go. He could get them another day. It was cold. He wanted to go home to his ma and his house and the warmth of the fire as the wind sang outside, carrying the smell of the Saturday night fry as he came in the gate. They went home to where G felt safe.

Four

The monastery was on the Greek island of Amorgos, clinging to the side of the cliff way above the sea, painted a pristine white and visible for miles against the black rock. They had visited when the sun was setting after a day spent swimming off the rocks. G, Ben and Lofty, bare-chested, the salt forming a crust on their skins.

At the door they were met by a monk swathed in black robes and a long grey beard which fell like a piece of rope onto his chest. There hung a silver crucifix studded with a bright blue stone which matched the monk's eyes.

Stepping in they felt the warmth of the sun on their backs disappear and the cool air brush their skin as they pulled on sweaters. As the doors were closed shut they got one last glance at the view behind them, sheet of glass for a sea, the sky a rainbow of colour, the sun painting strokes of crimson on the water as it went down.

They were led along the corridor by the monk, passing others who remained silent as they walked with heads bowed. They were given refreshments of light wine and olives and a brief tour of the monastery.

Some of the monks' cells were open, showing just a desk, a bed, a wardrobe and relics on the walls. The monastery was eight stories high and they had climbed 300 steps to get into it. It had a treasury and a kitchen with enough ovens to cook enough bread to both eat and sell and eat some more, storage rooms, cellars for wines, rooms for the earthenware jars full of sundried fruit, lime pits and wells for fresh water.

'Everything a man needs to live is here.'

'Except a woman.'

The monk had smiled at Lofty.

'We see women as a distraction from prayer and duty to God. That is all. It's a choice.'

'But you don't miss anything?'

'When you strip everything away, all that counts is what you need to live. Happiness comes from that. And, as you see, we have everything. We think about nothing else, so we don't miss it. Besides, goodness resides here with us. We feel safe.'

G never forgot that time, that place. He bought a postcard of the monastery at the island's harbour the day they left on the ferry and it was the only postcard he held on to after the month of travelling. And later that night, sitting outside one of the quiet bars along the harbour sipping beer and ouzo, they all swore they were going to turn their backs on the rat race for a time. That they would dedicate at least a year to pursue something radically different. It was a pledge made through the mind of adolescence, coupled with the incredible charm and beauty of the island they had found themselves on. It was easy to be fooled by beauty, Ben had said when they were on their way back to Athens. It wasn't that they had been fooled, G had said. They'd been captivated.

Lofty and Ben had eventually put that day behind them, that wish and that dream too. But G never had. And there was no better time to remind them. It had been four years. But none of them could have ever guessed the opportunity would come the way it did.

Overnight the sky fell down. From the US and across the Atlantic the shockwaves travelled to the tiny island that for so many years had been letting the good times roll without ever wondering when the wheels would come off and burn.

G recognised it when it came. Recognised it as an opportunity where other young students saw it as a calamity and the signal to escape. G had escape in mind, only not to anywhere very far away. When everything has been stripped bare, what is needed to live is all that counts. Happiness starts right there.

'Do you remember Greece? ,And that monastery we went to visit, up on the rocks?'

Ben looked at him.

'Why. Are you thinking of becoming a monk now?'

'What we talked about later that night, Ben. Remember?'

'We were drunk, if I remember correctly. And we were younger too.'

Lofty tore up an empty cigarette packet into small rectangles and stacked them like miniature bricks on G's kitchen table.

'It was special, wasn't it though? Built into the rock like that. And it was one of the best summers of my life.'

'That's what we all said. And it was too.'

Ben shook his head.

'So that's your plan, G? Go back over there? To do what? Greece was first to go, place is a mess.'

Lofty rearranged the cardboard bricks into four walls.

'I remember what we all talked about, so I do. We wanted to take a year out to do something different.'

Ben swore and stood and took three more cans of beer from the fridge, using one to sweep Lofty's creation aside.

'Yeah, something different, Lofty. That could have been anything. It was four years ago and if I remember, there was nothing concrete came out of it. Just . . . talk. Here we are weeks away from our last exams trying to decide what to do or where to go and G brings up monasteries.'

Lofty pulled the pieces back together with the palms of his hands.

'The future is not how we imagined it would be, Ben old boy. We don't have the same choices anymore.'

'So? We get out. Canada, Australia, America, wherever.'

G opened his can of beer and let it hiss.

'The monastery is only an analogy, Ben. It's got nothing to do with an actual monastery. It's what we need right now that counts.'

'We've been talking about bloody monasteries for the last hour, G.'

Lofty looked at G.

'So what you're saying G, is that you wish to start some sort of alternative lifestyle in the form of a community of... like-minded individuals. In a nutshell.'

'You should listen to yourself, Lofty.'

'Shut it, Ben—'

'We're not going to Greece, guys. Why would we go to Greece? We can do it right here,' G interrupted.

'Where?' Ben asked skeptically.

'Right here, in Ireland. We find the people first, on the campus. They must all be finishing this year, and they must all be prepared to give this at least twelve months.'

Ben shrugged and leaned back against the counter.

'And how are you going to convince them, G? 'Cos you haven't convinced me yet.'

'I'll convince enough of them, Ben. You'll see. We'll give it a year. Like we promised. One year. It's the perfect time to do something like this now. We've nothing to lose, because there is nothing else for us unless we get out altogether, just like you said, Ben. I'm not ready to do that yet.'

Ben looked imploringly at Lofty.

'You're not really thinking of this Lofty, you of all people. Tell me you're not. We were fooled back then, like I said. Fooled by the beauty of that place.'

'We were captivated, Ben. But let's not be fooled now. We need to make the right choice.'

Lofty threw a glance at G and swept the pieces of cardboard into the bin.

'What if I told you we had everything to lose, G.'

G shrugged.

'How do you mean everything? What have we got to lose? I've got nothing. Ben, don't think you've got much. And Lofty, I know you've certainly got nothing. So what have we got to lose?'

Ben pulled a seat out and sat down at the table.

'It can't work anyway, G. Economically even, it's a non-starter. Where are you going to get the place anyway? Where would you get the money? You just said we were all broke. Jesus, G, let's just get the fuck out. Anywhere is better than here right now.'

'I've already got a place.'

Lofty and Ben stared at him.

'And I've seen it. I've been there. And when you guys see it you are going to be struck with the same feelings that I was. It's as if it was waiting for us. And that's where we're going.'

Ben crushed his beer can slightly at the sides.

'Where is it? And who owns it?'

'A guy I met here in college, sort of by chance, but—'

'You were sort of meant to meet,' Ben finished for him.

'Maybe.'

'Typical.'

'Look, we've about two weeks to organise. Get some bodies together. We only need a handful of people. That's it. I've already had some serious requests. I'm doing it one way or another. So are we in?'

Ben looked over at Lofty.

'Did he tell you about this place, Lofty?'

'First I've heard.'

'So you've seen this place then, G?'

'I've been there. Spent a night there. It's perfect and it's ours for a year if we want it.'

Ben sighed.

'One year, G. I'm going to give you one year because, fuck it, we've always done things together. But I'm still not convinced.'

'Lofty?'

'Sure, G. Like you say, we've got nothing. So we've got nothing to lose.'

Five

'Believe it or not, there are over 3,000 instances of communal living in the Western World. That includes eco-villages, intentional communities, housing co-operatives and communes. Communal living comes from social and economic need, and now we all know there is a real need. Most of us sitting here today won't be able to afford our own homes. If we're lucky enough to get homes from parents, chances are we'll be paying for their mortgages. Only a handful of us here will be walking into a job after college and we'll have hefty loans to pay off that will probably take us all years.

'Ours is a simple experiment. We're going to restore a farm, from scratch, from the roots up and we're going to live on it. We're going to live on it and we're going to live from it. That's the challenge. One year from our lives. It's a social experiment and it's an economic experiment. We're going to be an independent, functioning eco-community with everything we need provided for right there on the land. This is not about protest, and it's not about dropping out. And it's not about leaving the country. It's about finding a new way of life for the times we are in.'

It was a minor hall in the old science wing used for smaller lectures and there was an echo in there, which gave off a sense of gravity. G liked the echo as he spoke. Gave him time to hear whether the words that came back were the right ones.

They came, of course they came. Just like G had said. Followed the signs on the Facebook page and whether through curiosity, boredom or a general need to find a way to pick through the gloom and doom that rained down daily, they came. Maybe not a lot, a hundred or so. But it was enough to deal with and plenty to choose from. There were other people offering other choices and the travel agency on campus was most appealing, with work Visas and flights and agents who could provide a list of manual jobs all as part of the package. There were more courses advertised on notice boards in the corridors and outside the lecture theatres and there were many even considering voluntary work for a year or so just to fill the time so the dust could settle. Then there was this guy offering them the chance to live on a farm for a year. The questions weren't long coming.

'What will you do if it works? I mean, beyond a year.'

'Those who want to stay can stay. And we turn it into an agri-business. We expand.'

'What do you do if it doesn't work? The business end of things, I mean. Trying to get a business off now is nuts.'

G sighed and leaned on the table in front of him.

'I know. I know all that. Which is why we look after ourselves first. If we can't do that, we leave. We leave and we find something else. We're only in our twenties. We won't have missed much. Look, whatever plans all of us had four years ago when we came to college, put them on ice. It's a very different world now. We just don't have the same choices.'

A guy sitting right under G's nose raised a hand.

'Have you even looked at the choices? If people keep running away there'll be even fewer options. And this isn't going to help anyone.'

'It will help us. And nobody is running away.'

'And what quality of life do you expect on a farm someplace?'

'Quality of life... what quality are you hoping for? What do you study?'

'Commerce. Economics major.'

'And you didn't see this coming? Well, what price do you put on your life?'

'What do you mean?'

'Well, let's put it this way. Say tomorrow, you were told you were terminally ill, and that you'll be dead within the year. But... you're also told there was a cure available. Now, how much would you pay for that cure?'

'Well, all I have I'm sure.'

'Yeah, but you've got nothing now. But would you be prepared to go into infinite debt to stay alive, having to give all you earn for the rest of your life – except of course a moderate sum for food and essentials – for that cure?'

'You're not comparing like with like here.'

'No, it's exactly the same problem. The quality of life for you wouldn't be good enough to agree to such a debt. But our generation is saddled with it. I don't want it. I'm sure nobody else in this room wants it. But we'll be paying to live like this for the rest of our lives. At least if we try something different for ourselves, we can decide what quality we have.'

'Which is?'

'When you strip everything away, what you really need to live is what counts. Happiness comes from that. Besides, goodness will reside with us. We can feel safe. Someone told me that once.'

There was a murmur which rose to a bit of a chant and a few heckles were thrown from somewhere down the back.

'Sounds like a communist.'

'No, he sounds like a monk.'

G shrugged and laughed.

'Fair enough.'

The same guy persisted.

'But there's still the economics of it.'

'Of course.'

'And you're still bound by the laws of this state. That includes rates and taxes and everything else.'

'Of course. Look, we're not rebels. There's no political motivation here. Like I said, it's an option driven by a basic need. Look at it as another choice.'

A girl halfway down the hall stood.

'How many places are there on this farm?'

'Between ten and fifteen. We can't do it with more because it wouldn't be manageable financially. And we can't do it with any less because of the amount of work involved.'

'And where is this farm?'

'Well, we can't reveal that at this time.'

'But you do have somewhere.'

G looked at Lofty and Ben, who each gave a small shrug.

'Well, it's like this —what's your name?'

'Joey.'

'Joey. There is a place, yes. It belongs to someone who has agreed to the project for a year. This other party is going to be fully involved and he is experienced. He's not here today.'

'Oh. Well it's all very covert and exciting at least.'

'Well, if you're interested in hearing any more, Joey, stay back later and we can discuss it. And of course, that goes for everyone. But please, if you're not interested, we just ask that you leave and forget about it. We don't really want that much attention, to be honest. We're off

Facebook already. That's down now until we're actually up and running in the real world. This is the first and last chance.'

The murmur began to rise again and G scanned the room once more, about to step down, when an older student stood and stopped him.

'All of these social experiments end in chaos. Have you not read *Lord of the Flies*? *Brave New World*? Violence broke out many times at Christiana in Copenhagen, you know. I was there.'

He looked around the room and extended an arm.

'Even if you find ten, fifteen people here today who agree with you, eventually, you'll realise people never want the same thing. That's where it all starts to go wrong.'

G stared hard at the guy.

'I understand where you're coming from. But we're only talking about a farm.'

'Farms are organic too, you know. They have ways of taking over the people that run them unless everything is very well controlled. Good luck but I won't be joining you.'

The hall doors swung and he was gone. Then came the sound of wooden chairs scraping on a concrete floor. G said nothing more. Climbed down off the podium and over to Lofty and Ben who sat at the sides.

Lofty stood and handed G a coffee in a plastic cup.

'Will we get the numbers, do you think? A lot of them are leaving.'

G sipped the coffee and eyed Joey and the business guy and a few others who had asked questions and were hanging back, finding the idea in itself enough to raise interest. When times were hard and people were getting desperate nothing can be more appealing than the basic offer of a roof over your head and a patch of land to call your own and do with as you please. It was what G had taken away from the farm after just the one night, and even if it was rough and needed a lot of work there was nothing like physical work either to make people feel like they're on the way to achieving something, especially on a farm where the end of every day shows some signs of having gotten something done, no matter how small.

And it was the first day of spring too, there was no better time to sell the idea of a farm than in spring, when the mornings were yellow instead of grey and the smell of cherry blossom hung in the air and the days were getting longer and the nights were being trimmed. There was no better time to sell the idea of a farm when all around there were signs of human failings. There was no better time to sell the idea of living off your own work when all around there were signs that money was failing and wasn't even worth working for anymore. There was no better time to sell the idea of living with friends and like-minded folk when all around there were signs they were packing up and leaving. And there was no better time to sell something that was free.

Six

G spent many a weekend with John on the farm over the next few weeks as spring tailed off into early summer. It was what they had agreed on after they had first bumped into each other and the notion of cooperation came up. John would spend some time showing G the ropes. He needed a right-hand man.

John had been one of the first to pick up on G's Facebook page. It had been sitting out there in the ether for several weeks and John had hooked it while fishing for assistance with the farm he had recently inherited. He needed financial assistance mainly. Legal assistance possibly. But what he hadn't counted on finding was someone out there looking for a farm. Looking for farm land at a time when you couldn't give it away. But that's what this guy wanted. G was all he called himself and he had a straightforward proposal. He was looking for someone who was willing to give over farmland in return for someone else to look after it at their expense. John saw the simple genius of it. Can't afford to live in your home for a couple of years, give it to someone who can until you're ready to take it back. Was there a term for it in the world of real estate? Who knows. John had land he couldn't afford to work and he was going to struggle to keep it before the banks moved in. So out there in the ether the twain did meet and the partnership was formed.

But G needed to learn. Learning that wouldn't seem like learning at first; stories about nature, customs, land and roots. But it was learning you wouldn't get in college. And you wouldn't get it in the city either. It was all about the senses which had to be sharpened.

The first thing John taught G was about smell. He said you could smell the countryside in many ways. And you would never get the same smells in the cities. Even cooking a good fry was different in the country because all the ingredients were fresher. He had shown G the size of the eggs he had bought for breakfast that first week they had come down. Eggs almost as big as a fist and a light brown, the colour of the sandy soil on the farm.

When John had stayed at the farm as a kid he would get the eggs fresh in the morning for his aunt, down in the chicken pen near the paddock. And in the evenings when he was working in the field, he'd smell the eggs and bacon and sausage as he walked back to the yard. There was nothing like it after a hard day working in the fields.

Then there was the smell of the fields themselves. Different scents for different seasons. Flowers in spring. Cut grass in summer. The cold muck in winter. And the smell of decaying leaves blowing in from the forest floor in autumn. Cows in the barn and their warm bodies smelling like new leather. The tomatoes swinging in the glasshouses like rows of tiny heads. People think tomatoes don't have a scent, but when there are hundreds of them in a glasshouse they have a smell like old bank notes. Then there was the smell of blood. Blood from a slaughtered pig, a sickly sweet smell that was unlike anything else you ever smelled before and you would never forget it once it left its impression on the senses. John had eventually discovered that the senses are the way to the mind and the way to the soul. And smell was a very powerful sense, more powerful than people gave it credit for. The animals used their sense of smell more than any other sense. And a strong smell would leave its imprint on the mind forever, as a sign and as a warning and as a means to identify things. And the smell of warm blood from a cut pig was unforgettable.

John had often killed pigs. They had a shed especially for slaughter, with long thin knives, a beam in the ceiling for roping the pig by his legs and a large bucket for the blood. He didn't like it too much, but he knew that he had to do it because that's what had always been done on a farm. He learnt that and accepted that it was just the way it was. What seemed cruel to some was necessity to others. Even hunting. And John took G hunting too using shotguns G had never even seen before. The closest thing he'd ever seen to it was an air rifle, which was still dangerous, but nothing like the shotguns John had on the farm. It had two barrels that took bright red cartridges and could rip the barn door from its hinges. John fired the rifle well. He was a big guy, well-built. G was thinner and lighter: sinewy, more athletic. The first shot kicked back like a mule and G thought he had knocked his shoulder out of its socket. He hadn't. But it felt bad. John told him that he would get used to it after a bit of practice. G wasn't so sure he wanted to practise. His shoulder hurt for days and there was a bruise that spread black and blue like ink on his skin.

But in all the time shooting, G never bagged a thing. John said he was missing on purpose. John got a rabbit one day. Blew it several feet in the air. Then he took a jack knife from his pocket and cleaned out its guts and skinned it right there in the field to show G how it was done. Didn't take him long either. And they had rabbit that evening stewed in a pot.

He blew a couple of pheasants out of the sky another day. G helped pluck them back in one of the sheds and he was going fine until he tore the stomach out. He almost retched with the smell but John told him it was a good thing that he was learning to use his nose.

John had managed to hold on to a small flock of sheep which he tended to with the help of two English sheep dogs housed in kennels near the stable. He also had a cow and two pigs on the farm which he had kept after he'd sold off all the other livestock. He wanted to hold on to those animals. Later he could get a bull and perhaps think about breeding. But right now, that cow would be good for milk. The pigs would be fed well over the coming months and slaughtered to make meat for the autumn, and even the winter if they managed well. And the sheep were there for meat and for their wool, and although it had never been done on his farm before, they could get milk and cheese from the sheep too. So taking it all into consideration, there was enough there for a small group of people to live off until well into the next year. And if they did things right over the summer and autumn, they would have new crops awaiting them by winter.

They would all have to do a lot of work by hand in the beginning, because so little of the machinery was left. But it would be good to get back to doing things by hand, and although it would be hard work, it would be rewarding. G had no objections to working the land.

He liked it out there with John. The first few days there was nothing but digging and turning soil on land that had been let lie and grow wild with every weed known to man. John would go first with a rotavator and G would go behind him with a spade and a rake pulling and scratching at the soil to leave nothing but pure brown earth. Nothing else could be in there before they planted. No leaves, no roots; nothing. But things came up out of that earth that G had no idea where they came from. Not just rocks and the roots of stubborn thick weeds, but manmade objects too. Buried at some time in the past or lost by a child. Coins, heads and limbs of toy dolls, an old leather boot that G took inside to clean up and fill with the clean soil. Then he planted a cutting of a rosemary in it to see would it grow because rosemary was his favourite herb with meat.

He found a key one morning too. Looked like a key to a dresser or cabinet and John kept it, sure he would find its home some place in the house, or up in the attic or in one of the old sheds. He cleaned it up with sandpaper and put it on a piece of string, then hung it on a nail just inside the kitchen door.

When they weren't digging up the earth they were putting things back into it and they were pulling stuff out of it too that was ready to be stored as food.

There were potatoes that had to be picked before

they rotted in the ground. And G's back was stiff and hurt like hell at the end of a day doing that. There were seeds to be planted so vegetables would be available for them all to live off. The glasshouses would have to be weeded. The paddock had to be cut and grass stored for feed and compost. The apple trees pruned. The sheds cleaned out and the barn swept. There was a job every day and it was never going to be all done until the help arrived. But G and John spent all the time they could that month of June in the rain and the sun and never stopped toiling.

In the evening, they'd light a fire in the barnyard and talk until they grew too tired, then they'd just watch the orange sky rinse with black as night came down and they'd fall asleep, the sounds of the countryside ringing in their ears.

Ben and Lofty came down on the weekends that first month. But they didn't take to the work as quickly as G had done. Ben was just that bit overweight, that bit cumbersome. He complained when he couldn't get the hang of something and would continue complaining until someone stopped him. Eventually John put him in the glasshouses weeding out the aisles and de-leafing the bottom half of the tomato plants.

Ben hated that. He said he'd just finished a Science degree and had never heard of de-leafing tomato plants, bottom or top. John would say that no degree in the world would prepare him for things that could happen on a farm, and de-leafing tomato plants was just the start of it all.

So Ben would do the job John told him to do. And he'd do it well. Because Ben was a proud guy, despite his temperament. He hated to think you'd be talking about him going back on things. So he'd sit there in the warm clay with the heat under the glass rising by the hour, stripping the leaves from the bottom of the plants until his hands were green and his legs cramped up. Then at the end of an aisle he'd stand and straighten himself and look back at the gaunt skeletal figures with their small red heads bowing over in the heat of the glasshouse. And he'd have to repeat the process with the next aisle.

But he never asked why he was doing it. And John never told him either. Just said it had to be done. So Ben worked at it, and he even began to notice that tomatoes had a strange smell, all of their own. And when he entered the glasshouse early in the morning he noted how much stronger the smell was then, compared to the evening when he was leaving. He liked that smell. Welcomed it. It smelled like old money. Then things got easier for him.

Lofty was more enthusiastic but lacked the real physique needed to do much of the manual work. He was tall, gangly almost, and always seemed to wear the wrong clothes. It was as if he had never known what a farm was and what it meant to be on one. He'd wear his black blazer round the place during the day, the same one he wore in college. When it got dirty he'd look at it as if he was surprised that it had gotten spoiled. He'd wear clean jeans and shoes and his thin-framed glasses were always about to fall off his narrow face. He'd cut himself. Get bruises. Slip and fall over. And he'd get confused. But instead of moaning like Ben, he'd laugh and keep going.

John finally got him some work clothes, a pair of baggy dungarees that Lofty eventually grew to love. They hung off his thin body and made him look like a scarecrow. John said he was going to come in handy looking like that and they could stuff him with straw and stick him out in the fields. But Lofty scoffed at that suggestion. Was there really such thing as a scarecrow that did its job? And John agreed. Those crows were afraid of nothing. They had become too clever to be afraid of a stuffed figure standing in the middle of a field. But very often scarecrows did a job they weren't supposed to do, which was scare people. John told them of several occasions where his uncle had put out the first scarecrow of the year without John knowing it. And when he was walking back in from the fields as it was getting dark, he would come over the brow of the hill and there against the blackened horizon was a figure with its arms splayed out as if crucified. Straw that looked like broken bones protruded from the sackcloth and two eyes made from pieces of coal were stuck into a gaunt face. The wind would move the tall crops around it, but the scarecrow would stand still.

John grew to hate the scarecrows his uncle made every year. And when the time came to take them down he'd light a big fire and put the scarecrow at the top. Then he'd sit there alone and watch it burn.

Seven

John had to light a fire even though it was the end of June. He went into the trees with an axe and chopped up some deadfall that was lying around on the floor of the forest. Then he packed the logs into a wheelbarrow and rolled it up to the back door.

Some of the logs went into the kitchen for fuel for the old Aga cooker. The rest went up to the front room where Ben and Lofty sat, complaining about the cold; Lofty in the rocking chair that creaked as he rocked and Ben on a hard stool pulled up in front of the hearth, warming a whisky in a glass over the coals.

'I always put ice in my whiskey. But the last thing I want now is ice.'

Then he drank the whiskey neat, in small sips.

And it was that cold the first evening, the evening the rest of the group were due to arrive. Ben and Lofty had come down the night before and after helping prepare the rooms and the rota for the first month, sat in the living room waiting.

G was out walking, over in the far fields that were wild and rarely visited. They were thick with tall grass and weeds as big as small trees and on this evening covered with a film of vapour from a mist which floated in over the hills. He had stood and watched it for some time until eventually it swallowed the forest, then the paddock, the glasshouses, and eventually drifted up to the edge of the lawn where he stood, swirls of mist licking his boots. There was something about that mist which gave the farm that he had grown to love in such a short space of time a very different image. That worried him, because the group were all arriving, and most for the first time. He didn't want them to get a bad impression the first night. He had hoped for one of those warm clear summer evenings which turns the sky cherry red and they could sit outside and watch the stars appear and light a bonfire of chopped wood. But it wasn't to be.

As G walked up to the steps of the farmhouse to the door he caught a glimpse of two yellow lights off on the hills in the distance, near where he'd been walking. It stopped. The light spread like buckshot in the drizzle of mist and there was a throb of an engine, a low hum like a tractor or an ageing SUV. He watched and it watched back but neither would have seen any detail. But that connection was there for almost a minute until the yellow eyes went into a dip in the field then turned and over out of sight. Then he felt the fingers of mist behind him. So he moved quickly inside to the fire, and out of the cold that was unusual for that month of the year.

It had been arranged that everyone should come down without giving any details to friends or family other than they were going away for the summer to work with a college friend to get the farm that he had inherited in shape. That was the story and there was a kernel of truth in it. They were helping John with the farm. He didn't have enough funds and no bank would loan him more money to try and breathe life into a holding that for the last few years had been a failure.

It wasn't just John's farm that was failing to balance the books. John said he had seen the shadows of men cast up and down the countryside as they turned their backs and walked away from their land. Many of his neighbours had gone and the land was just abandoned. He could feel the emptiness, the warmth of men around him vanish. Some had done nothing to deserve what they got, merely stood their ground and worked as they always had done. Others had prospered and made their fortunes. Sold up land banks for mad money to developers who had dreams of building on them. But they didn't build communities, they buried them.

'Ghost towns, man. See the tumbleweed blowing through the streets of some of the places I passed through today. Ballaghaderreen, Strokestown, Tulsk,

Ballymackfuck, could barely get a coffee anywhere. Businesses boarded up. Would hate to have to lay me head down in this part of the world. Came to one hotel which had no water. Doors were closed. Imagine? Staff sent home, and the notice was over three weeks old! I was starving by the time I got here.'

Matt took a bite out of the sandwich John had put together. Meat burst out at the sides.

'Where did everything go? Had to have gone somewhere.'

He spat breadcrumbs and more clung to his lips, so he grabbed a pint glass of cider to wash them away.

'You're one of the last few cowboys, John. But you mightn't be in the shit you're in now if you'd have sold up.'

'Things work in cycles, Matt. The good times will come around again. If that's what you want to call what happened here the good times. I prefer the way things were when I was a kid on this place. Nobody was rich. Nobody was poor. We all had good times, though without giving it much thought.'

'Unbelievable.'

Matt licked his fingers and rolled a cigarette so fast it was like it came from his sleeve. He offered it round but heads shook so he stuck it in his mouth and pulled a zippo from the pocket of his ex-navy jacket then leaned against the mantelpiece ready to tip the ash onto the coals.

The front door slammed and the sitting room door swung open. G entered rubbing his hands.

'Matt. Good to see you, mate. You got here first.'

'About half-an-hour ago.'

'How was the drive?'

'Sucked. Just telling the guys here. Like Mad Max wasteland.'

'Did you get something to eat.'

'John made me a sandwich with —what was it John?'

'Meat.'

Matt shrugged and tipped tobacco flakes into the fire.

'Did the job.'

'You're on your own, then?'

'The rest are on the bus, I hear. Offered a lift but got no takers. Suppose I wouldn't take a lift in my car either.'

The initial target was autumn, by which time they would have enough food stored and more crops planted to get them through the winter. The following spring would see them expand with the possibility of taking on more hands, since the summer would see them cultivate twice the amount of crops than they had the previous year. John would be working on selling some produce and there were other ideas to bring in a modest income to support their needs. But he was under no illusions about a viable business with the economic climate the way it was. Logically, if farmers were going out of business all around him, then with the amount of free labour at his disposal and the capacity to produce a large turnover of crop, then he should be able to enter the market at a competitive rate. But it hinged on so many factors, many he was prepared not to share with anyone, not even G, until he had a better idea of how the future shaped up.

His first priority was to rebuild. Renovate the buildings, work the land and get it into shape to give him the edge on farmers who were struggling, unable to pay labour, unable to expand. As far as finances were concerned, he had some money from selling machinery. He had paid some of the debt. And all the members of the group had contributed to a seed money fund. It wasn't a lot, but between them they had managed to gather almost €5,000. The banks would be on him, it was only a matter of how long. But if he could be scratching some sort of income when the time came to declare his status and that of the farm, then he might be able to hold them off.

G approached the fire and held the palms of his hands out. He kicked his boots off on the hearth.

'That normal, John? The mist out there. Bloody cold too.'

'It has been warm so a cold snap is bound to bring it in, yeah…' John mused.

A log popped in the fire and an ember spat onto the wooden floor. Matt plucked it up with the tongs and lobbed it towards the back.

'Global warming.'

'I know Matt,' said G. 'That's another reason for being here. We should go down the town and meet the rest. They'll never find this place on a night like this. What do ye all think?'

Lofty's chair creaked.

'I think we should just wait, G.'

Ben got up from the stool now that Matt had moved in front of him.

'We found it all right,' he stated.

'You've been here before though.'

'We found it then, G. Jesus, what has you so worried? They're probably in the boozer.'

'We said no pubs. Don't want to attract attention.'

Matt laughed and flicked the butt of his cigarette into the fire.

'Wouldn't worry too much. This town is dead.'

John stood and grabbed the plastic bin that was full of ice and cider bottles and spun it in small circles so it stood in the centre of the room.

'Will you stop talking about things being dead, Matt. We came up here to feel alive. I don't want you spouting that shit when the rest of them come in.'

He grimaced as he submerged his hand up to the elbow in ice and pulled out a bottle just as there came the sound of feet on the concrete steps outside and a knock on the front door. And with that cold hand he shook the hands of those who entered his home, the home of his uncle and the generations before them, who had worked through every season to keep the land in their hands and not entrust it to outsiders. But here they were and John welcomed them all one by one past the threshold because now times had changed and he needed the help of others one way or another. And so by the early hours of the morning the house was quiet, the people sound asleep and the fire a deep red glow in the hearth with the fox heads at either end of the grate in shadow.

Despite the fact that they were all alone in this huge place, with acres of land surrounding them outside and corridors drenched in darkness inside; despite the sounds of the nocturnal animals out in the fields and the wind blowing in gusts; despite the branches of trees tapping on the windows and the floorboards that creaked all by themselves, they slept like the dead.

Eight

G shivered and grimaced as he got up and stepped barefoot onto the wooden floor which was covered over with dust and splinters. He'd been sanding the floors upstairs, himself and John, over the last week and whitewashing them along with the walls, figuring it was the easiest colour to deal with and now the whole upstairs from the landing down the corridor and each bedroom reeked of fresh paint and wood shavings.

It was after midday and downstairs there was a buzz in the main room and a steady flow of traffic between the bathrooms and the kitchen. It had been a late night, the first part of it spent arguing about the group's tardiness, the second part getting drunk. Not that it was really divided that equally. In fact there was probably more time spent getting drunker than they already were when they arrived having spent a good part of the evening in one of the bars. It was near five o'clock when the last head found a place to rest and the sun not far away behind the hills either. But it didn't interfere with their sleeping when it found them. They slept like the dead the whole bunch of them.

They had argued though. One side saying they should have gone straight up and not attracted any attention and the other saying they'd got away with it as the pub wasn't very full and it was only for a couple of hours to warm up and get some food and drink and wait for the mist to clear. Couldn't see a thing in that mist that rolled straight down off the hills and covered the roads like steam. But G had said there was plenty of food and drink on the farm. And wasn't it one of the reasons they were all coming in the first place. But he admitted the mist had made him uneasy too and eventually he gave in.

Now it was time to find their way around the house and the farm and go through the list that had been compiled for the tasks they were all assigned to. Nobody knew what it was they were going to do but there many with preferences, all ready to give voice to them on that first morning. It was decided that G and John would assign tasks since they were the ones who had spent the majority of time down on the farm preparing things, so they were the ones who knew what had to be done. And it wasn't going to be a question of preferences either.

'The first priority is building and renovating the old workers' outhouses. We're going to need that space. And Terry, you're in charge of organising that.'

Terry scratched at stubble he had decided to leave for another day. Then he shrugged a pair of stocky shoulders visible through a t-shirt that hugged his torso. Terry was an obvious choice to have in the first batch. His dad was a contractor, one of the good guys, he always said, and he had spent three summers in London working the sites. He had plans to follow his father into the business, but there wasn't much of a business left to go into. He was keen to be given charge of renovating the outhouses and had blagged some power tools and equipment a few weeks previously. G had never asked where.

'I'm going to start with the painting and redecorating inside, G, if you don't mind. Starting with that awful wood chip paper down here. My first aim is to bring a bit of cheer into the house. We've got nice warm but neutral colours. Nothing fancy, nothing cold, just nice. I'm going to need a crew of about four for the next couple of weeks. After that there is a bit of repair work in the house, nothing major, a few floorboards here, a couple of dodgy sticky there, stuff that myself and Pete can do in about a week.'

He gave a nod to the guy beside him who said nothing and sipped his tea.

'We can use Matt too. Good arms on him.'

Matt lifted his arms above his head, a rolled-up cigarette in between two fingers.

'Fine by me.'

'Then it's on to the big job, like you say, which is to get those old outhouses into shape. That should take us up to September, I reckon. Maybe October.'

G nodded. Tapped the clipper board he held in his hands with the biro, found the next name on his list, then used the biro to locate them in the room.

'Joey. I believe you've been promised the glasshouses and the vegetable gardens?'

Joey was eating muesli. The clang of the spoon on the bowl filled the room.

'Mmm. That's right.'

'That's just as important as the lodgings, Joey, so you can get cracking on it. Ben's been in the glasshouses already cleaning the place up. But it's up to you now to take over. John will go through it with you.'

'Of course. And I'm taking Sara and Colm – Butcher as you call him – away from you too.'

'I had Butcher in mind for something else actually.'

'Well you can't. He's mine.'

G glanced at John who shrugged and gave a half nod, then he looked at the small guy with a head of curls gazing through the window.

They needed a butcher, despite protests from some of the group uncomfortable with the notion of having to slaughter and butcher animals. But it was part of the process and John had assured them that it would be an occasional rather than a frequent event. He had done it. His uncle had done it. And now they would have to do it.

'Is that okay there, Butcher?'

'What?'

'You didn't hear a word. Joey is taking you for the glasshouses as well, so you'll be busy. But this morning, you're teaming up with John, going through poultry, sheep, meat stocks, storage and all the rest.'

'Pigs.'

'The pigs. And John will show you that ghastly shed he has at the bottom of the paddock with the beam and the knives.'

Joey's muesli spoon stopped clanking.

'G, some of us here are vegetarians. Can you spare us?'

'We've discussed all of this and we're not doing it again now.'

'Well, I'd rather it wasn't discussed in front of me, G. And I won't be calling him Butcher either.'

John sat on the arm of the couch and leaned into the circle.

'Folks. Let's be blunt about this. We're all going to have to pitch in to every task that needs to be done here. Whether that involves sweating in greenhouses or wringing the necks of chickens, it'll all have to be done. If anyone has any sensitivities then they'll have to examine them quick. G has been here with me a while now and he can tell you all about the workload and about—'

G stopped him with a hand on his shoulder.

'Okay. We won't be wringing necks today. But there is one thing while we're talking about all this stuff that we got to heed from day one. Some of you have met Brian and some of you haven't. Either way, we're grateful to have him. Doc? A few words?'

Doc closed the book he'd been leafing through.

'I'm preparing a talk on safety issues around the farm. I'll be ready in a week or so and will go through everything then, myself and John. But all I will say right now, before anyone goes out that door, every job, every little task, has to be done carefully. I've qualifications and some experience in the field. But not these fields. I'm as green on this farm as everyone else.'

Sara looked at him as she blew steam from the surface of her mug of tea.

'What kind of things are we looking out for, exactly?'

'Well, like I said, I'll be going through it all in detail. But no one should use tools or machinery of any kind until we know about them back to front. Otherwise, use your common sense. Animals bite. Bees sting. Branches fall from trees. People fall off ladders. Watch your step. Finally, and I'm not open to discussion on this, what I say goes. Think of me as the health and safety officer on a building site. If I say down tools, then it's down tools.'

Matt squashed his butt on a saucer spilling ash on to the wooden floor.

'And that means inside too, Matt.'

Doc nodded and went back to his book.

'Next up. All cooking is going to be done on a rota. But we still need someone to keep the kitchen in order and there's the office and admin. Someone's got to do those. Any takers?'

Sara nodded.

'I can do the kitchens, G. I can divide the time between the glasshouses and vegetables with the kitchen. I mean, if I'm working with the food every day I might as well keep stock as well. Joey can help out.'

'I'll be busy enough outside, Sara, thanks very much. You love cooking. You'll be fine.'

G shook his head.

'It's not just cooking, Joey. You can help her. And

like I said, we're doing it on a rota. Two at a time. It'll be posted in the kitchen That includes cleaning and everything else that's needed to be done. Thanks Sara. Now, the office? Jane?'

Jane glanced up, a strand of hair dyed an off-red wrapped around her finger. She let it go then shrugged.

'Can you handle the office? Part-time. It just needs a few hours a week.'

'Sure.'

'You don't mind?'

'Why would I mind?'

The sun suddenly got the better of a cloud and light spilled into the room. Hands, magazines, hats and plates shielded eyes and the room emptied, leaving only G and Jane.

'Do you want to see the office?'

'Sure.'

It was darker and cooler at the back of the house and Jane walked first into the office and stopped at the large oak desk. She traced the grain in the wood with her fingers and drew a small circle with a nail.

'Same colour as your hair, G.'

'Nice.'

'And your eyes.'

'Nice again.'

'And—'

'Okay, Jane. Leave all that. What happened your own hair?'

'You preferred blonde?'

'Gentlemen do.'

'Since when were you ever a gentleman? Do you not think they'll call this favouritism?'

'Just a few hours a week, Jane. Accounts, website when it's up, stock. All that. John has some files ready for you to input. But I think he's sloppy, Jane. With the finances. I need someone I know well to go through them with a fine tooth comb. See where we're at here.'

G nodded at the few cardboard boxes at Jane's feet.

'You didn't answer my first question, G.'

'No, they won't think it's favouritism. And so what if they do? It's my call. Besides, it's been a while, hasn't it?'

'Six months.'

'Thereabouts.'

'No. Six months.'

Jane sat down into the large chair at the desk and swung around on it, smiling up at G.

'You've probably thought of everything here G, have you?'

'I hope so. I really do.'

Jane nodded and pulled open a drawer on the desk randomly. There was a letter opener. A heart made of copper hugged by two hands made of silver. She prodded the tip of her finger with the point then ran the edge along her palm and leaned over and leafed through a sea of envelopes in one of the boxes, scanning the postal marks and raising an eyebrow.

'Most of these are going to be from people waiting for answers, G. Has John given you many answers?'

'I've been limiting my questions to certain subjects, Jane. Look, he's said he's up to it in debt. We just need to know how bad, that's all. Before we get in too deep.'

Nine

G swung the hammer and hit the nail dead centre, driving the wooden frame that John had made for their manifesto into the wall on the hall for the group to see when they came back in that evening.

Goals and Rules

1. The farm is to maintain the values of the small business and to avoid the trappings of agri-business. Through agriculture, we can achieve self-sufficiency. Through growing our own food we can achieve a connection with each other and with the land. Our aim is to eat meat that is reared here on the farm only. We understand that the killing of animals is necessary to provide meat for those who wish to eat it. From our fields only, that is to be our rule for everything.

2. The farm must exist within the laws of the State. It cannot be our intention to provoke the State into a response that will endanger our project.

3. The farm will depend on benefiting from each other's knowledge and will therefore encourage learning and sharing of knowledge through classes so we can learn skills necessary to our survival. This is vital if we are to expand and we expect everyone to take part.

4. The farm can take applications from new members once a period of twelve months has elapsed and the project has, in the opinion of all members, been deemed a success. The inductee will be subject to a probationary period of three months during which s/he will be assessed by his/her peers. On completion of the three-month period the inductee will be subject to a vote by all members of the farm.

5. The farm is to maintain a secular belief in human values and is not to be subject to rules based on religion, foreign cultures or traditions. People are free to follow their conscience in matters of religious faith but cannot expect the group as a whole to obey religious observances. Any new members are forbidden therefore, to try and indoctrinate others with religious beliefs and customs. Religious attire and the wearing of religious symbols is also strictly forbidden. However, individuals are free to keep religious paraphernalia among their private possessions.

6. Anyone who breaks the rules of the farm will face instant dismissal regardless of the wishes of any of his/her peers.

That first day had been a warm one, despite the chilly morning, and the afternoon stretched into a pink evening as people began slowly winding down after their first day of physical labour.

G went outside into the paddock and stretched himself out in the long grass, grass up to his knees in length. He pulled a large blade out of the ground, snapped off the hairy root between thumb and forefinger and began to chew on the pale green shoot.

He stared out across the distant fields, taking off his jumper and rolling it up for a pillow. Lying back, he inhaled the warm air and realised just how good he felt watching the clouds float by above his head, slowly, without any urgency and without any effort, as if screened from a projector.

After half an hour or so he sat up again and looked out across the fields. Everyone was weary, dragging their boots sodden with wet clay back towards the house. Terry and Peter, tops off, were walking back from the outhouses. Out beyond the barn, Joey and Sara were leaving the glasshouses, caked in sweat, their hair stuck to their faces.

G spat out the piece of grass just as he spotted Lofty out at the river, so he called out to him and Lofty turned, holding his hand up against the low sun, then broke into a bit of a trot. He stood over G catching his breath.

'Have you been just sitting here all day?'

'Not all of it.'

Lofty rested his hands on his knees and pulled a water bottle from the side pocket of his dungarees.

'Well, I've been working on cleaning out those outhouses. Just went over to the river there. Cold water on the feet is a great way of easing them.'

'Give us your verdict then? What are they like, those buildings?'

Lofty sat, crushing the grass.

'Why? Have you not been in them yourself? You've only been here… what, weeks?'

G glanced quickly at Lofty.

'Can't stand the sight of those things. Dark, damp. Cobwebs everywhere. Christ.'

'I wouldn't live in them myself G, to be honest. Not yet anyway.'

Lofty propped his glasses back on his nose as he swigged from the water bottle, rinsed then spat.

'But those boys seem to know their stuff. They might surprise us when they get round to doing them up. But the state they're in now. There's bloody spiders in there, G – I'm not joking – the size of my hand.

He held his hand out.

'And I've big hands.'

G looked at Lofty's hand and shook himself a bit. Spiders, large as rats. Spiders so big they could eat birds. Eat those crows even that hung around over the fields even.

'Well, we'll decide who is going in there later. The girls wanted them so I hear. They can have them. I'm scared shitless of spiders. Where's Ben?'

'Helping Butcher with the cow the last I looked.'

'The cow? Sure Ben wouldn't know the difference between a cow and a bull for God's sake.'

'Well, he'll have to learn. He's on milk collection in the mornings with Butcher and John. And we're all getting on that roster eventually, so don't laugh. And then there's the pigs. One of them is going to get the chop soon. That'll be fun.'

G looked over towards the barnyard where John had fenced off a patch of grass that was now muck from two pigs pulling the clay asunder with their snouts.

'Ben getting milk. That's a good one. As for those pigs, well, that's Butcher's job.'

'We're all part of it, G. Sorry, old boy. And John is saying that when the time comes, we've all to go through it.'

G looked back at the pigs. He could hear them, grunting as they rolled. He had yet to figure out what sex they were because he had yet to go within a hundred yards of them. They looked happy as a pair, whatever they were. It was going to be a real challenge pulling one of the poor animals out for slaughter, and G didn't want to be anywhere near that ghastly shed when it happened.

Lofty stood and brushed the back of his dungarees down with his hands.

'Tell me, G, how did you swing this place, really?'

'Never look a gift horse and all that Lofty.'

'But why would John want to do something like this? I mean property prices will creep back up and there'll be a demand for land again. Besides, he was sitting on a fortune here. Even if it is in the middle of nowhere.'

'You're missing the fundamental here, Lofty.'

'What's that?'

'Not everyone wanted the boom. Especially in rural places like out here. Not everyone wanted the changes. They were happy enough doing what they were doing. John was one of them. And I imagine a lot of the people here felt the same way. And you're forgetting something else.'

G stood and put his arm around Lofty's shoulder and began walking back towards the barn.

'What's that then?'

'Roots, Lofty.'

'Roots? What are you talking about?'

'You'll find out Lofty. He needed us as much as we wanted him. You can be sure of that. Do you think he could afford to employ people to do what we're doing? Tax-free too.'

They had supper of eggs, beans and a meatloaf that John had made that afternoon in a rectangle backing tin blackened and encrusted at the sides. After supper they sat at the large table, one half sitting in the whitewashed alcove, the rest with their backs to the windows as dusk sank in and around them.

Matt picked at the baking tin with his fork.

'What was in the meatloaf, John?'

'Meat.'

Matt put the fork down.

'Did the job.'

Terry leaned forward, grabbed the teapot and poured out seconds.

'Are we going to make the targets, John?'

John looked down at the list square in the centre of the table that they had all been going through. There was a lot more work to be done than they had first anticipated. John's guess was that it would take them well into autumn to have it out of the way. It was a late deadline. They had expected things to be ready end of August. But there was too much to do and there was a lot more to do that they didn't know had to be done. Things even that were discovered on that first day by people once they had got their hands dirty and realised it wasn't going to be an easy time of it. Things even John hadn't figured out fully.

Fences had to be repaired around the perimeter and up in the far fields where sheep could wander and fall into any kind of hole or a marsh or a river and die. The interior of the house needed the attention that Terry had said it needed. The outhouses were a priority for more sleeping and living space once the main house was done. The glasshouses had to be maintained and tomatoes watered and picked and deleafed regularly. The winter vegetables had to be put in the ground soon. If worst came to worst they could almost live the whole winter on them. Broad beans, spinach, onions, peas, winter lettuce and cabbage. They could make stews and soups for weeks on that.

Then there were the henhouses to be patched up to keep hens that John and Butcher were going to buy in the markets in the coming weeks to get them eggs. The barn had to be renovated. One of the pigs had to be slaughtered and meat prepared for store. The list was endless. And it meant every day being used to the full and every night getting proper amounts of sleep. The autumn deadline was going to put pressure on them for winter, and the winter would bring its own issues that no one apart from John really knew anything about.

'We'll get there. Don't you worry your little heads.'

'Just don't want to starve, John. I've not got a penny left to me name.'

'You won't starve, Terry. And if you're worried, wait until I get my poitín out. You'll have nothing but the nicest possible thoughts then.'

Matt looked into his mug of tea.

'Get it out now, sure.'

G stood and began putting dishes into the large earthenware sink beneath the window.

'Not tonight, Matt. We're up early.'

Matt yawned.

'Man, I'm tired. When are we going to take a break? Get a lie-in, some down time. Jesus.'

G ran the tap mixing hot and cold, only there was more cold than hot, and Jane and Joey joined him at the sink washing up and drying and putting everything back in the cupboards. Then they cleaned the counters, swept the floor and put the rubbish outside in the bins, and then got the clean bowls and mugs down on the table ready for breakfast the next morning, all in accordance with the roster. Then as they made their way up the stairs the clock in the hall began to chime ten times, only by the time it reached ten they were already in bed.

Ten

Terry and Pete worked hard every minute they had but they were hampered by the demands of Joey and Sara over the paintwork inside the house. They had hit their target with the repairs and had put up shelves and wardrobes in the rooms. They'd sealed up draughts and windows against the cold that would be inevitable come autumn. And they had even begun putting in an extra shower and toilet in one of the rooms after there had been so many arguments in the mornings and particularly in the evenings when people were growing cold waiting for hot showers after sweating in the fields all day.

With regard to the painting, Terry and Pete, as they had said at the first meeting, had gone and played it safe, choosing tins of a simple cream matt for the walls of every room and a white gloss for the skirting boards and doors. But when the girls saw the colours they called a stop before the hallway was touched, which Terry was about to do early one morning.

Joey stood on the bottom step arms folded and Sara on the step above with her head in her hands and her elbows on her knees.

'Are we going to be wearing uniforms too then?'

'What does that mean, Joey?'

'It means, Terry, that if everything is going to look the same, then we might as well too.'

Terry looked at Pete, who shrugged and put down his brush and leaned the step ladder against the wall and walked downstairs to the kitchen.

'You sort that out, Terry. Do you want a cup of coffee?'

'No. Yes, get us a cup of coffee.'

He gazed around at the walls of the hall which had been painted a canary yellow but had soured over the years and had blackened towards the ceiling.

'You don't want to smother the hall in colour, Joey.'

'You don't want it to be too clinical either, Terry.'

'For Christ's sake. Okay, Joey, let's get everyone together and see what they think.'

There was a bell over the list of rules that G had put up. Matt said it was for last orders. G called it a rallying bell to be rung when everyone was to come together. It was loud too, but maybe not loud enough to be heard down the fields. So John was getting another outside at the kitchen door for that purpose.

Terry grabbed the chain and the bell rung out throughout the hall and into the rooms and up into the rafters in the attic where John was down on his hands and knees looking through boxes and chests that hadn't been looked through in years.

'Jesus.'

He stood then stooped low to climb down the ladder and G who was in his bedroom heard it too and he swore and went down the stairs. And Jane, who was in the office up to her knees in paperwork, swore and went out into the hallway. Lofty, Ben and Doc, who were all outside in the outhouses about to get started on sanding the walls, heard it too, downed tools and in they went. Eventually, everyone was gathered in the hall staring at the tins of paint with Pete beside them calmly doing his best to explain the choice of colour but starting to lose it as Joey just sat rigid on the steps of the stairs and shook her head.

'It's boring, Pete.'

'It's a simple case of practicality and economy, Joey.'

He sipped his coffee and stared at Joey over the top of the mug.

'Do you get it? We chose a neutral colour because it will go with everything, the walls and the floors, the furniture, the lot. And it means we can get it done quickly.'

'It's boring. We just think it's boring.'

Terry scratched somewhere between his shoulder blades.

'Well, what colour would you like? Red? Bright red? Pink?'

Sara gazed up at the ceiling

'No, not red.'

She stared hard at the tins of paint on the floor squinting as if trying to will the colour to change itself.

'Red is too powerful and it can also… have an effect on blood pressure and respiration.'

'Oh, Jesus Christ.'

Terry took his mug of coffee from the hall table and sat on the stairs too.

'See, this is why we didn't bother getting carried away with colour. Psychology graduates. So what other colours will freak us out, Sara?'

'It's not really a question of getting freaked out, Terry. There are different effects. Yellow causes fatigue, purple is spiritual, black is submissive, so we need comfort colours, like orange or green. Or maybe even a shade of blue.'

Joey nodded in agreement.

'Blue works.'

Terry looked up at the others.

'What do you say, Jane? Or am I going to be hung now for thinking this is a sexist issue we have going on here?'

Jane shrugged indifferently.

'I'm easy. But I think we're going to have a lot of fun sorting this out.'

John suddenly moved down from the top of the stairs pushing a couple of bodies aside.

'Okay. This is going to drive me mad. I personally would whitewash the whole bloody place like we did upstairs. And that's what I'm going to do if we don't reach an agreement by midday.'

Butcher raised his hand.

'Is there any way we could draw lots or something?'

Joey raised her eyes to the ceiling which was flaking at the corners.

'And how would you do that?'

Butcher reddened.

'Put colours in a hat?'

Matt put his hands on the walls and let them linger.

'We could always just leave the walls as they are. Sort of organic vibe. At least there'd be no arguments over colour.'

Ben sighed and shook his head.

'That's because there would be no colour.'

There was a creak from the living room where Lofty sat in his rocking chair watching through the open door.

'I go with the guys anyway.'

Doc pushed people aside and moved away down the hallway but Ben put an arm out to stop him.

'Where are you off to, Doc?'

'Back outside.'

'But we've got to sort this shit out.'

'Sort it out then.'

G swore under his breath and walked to the centre of the hall and lifted one of the tins of paint and examined the label closely.

'I have to agree that this colour is a bit dry.'

Terry threw him a stare.

'At the same time, apart from painting every room a different colour, one colour for each person, I don't see any other way out of it.'

Butcher nodded and raised his hand.

'That's not a bad idea. And we can draw lots, like I said.'

Ben laughed.

'How do we do that?'

Butcher began counting his fingers.

'There are twelve of us. So, we choose a colour each and put the rooms into the hat. Then we pick a room each and whatever room each of us get, well, we paint it the colour of our choice.'

Terry ran his fingers through his hair.

'That's mad.'

'But at least it's fair.'

'I don't care, Joey. It's mad. And we're the ones doing the painting here and we've other stuff to be getting on with too.'

'Let's decide on only warm colours for the social rooms, the living room and kitchen, cool colours for the bathrooms and you can do what you like everywhere else.'

'Christ.'

There was a long silence, broken only by the sound of Terry scratching his scalp.

'Go for it. You win.'

Other upsets loomed over those first few weeks. They found their way in through the smallest of splits in the circle. There were rows over rooms. Some faced east and had the light of the summer sun at five thirty in the morning, waking the ones who slept there. Others faced west and were darker in the morning but warmer in the evenings from the heat of the sun during the day. The kitchen rota was a disaster. Some people couldn't cook, served up beans and toast and bacon at the end of a long day. Others made shepherd's pie, curry, bean casseroles and stews. They used their imagination with leftovers so nothing went to waste. They cleaned up and took stock regularly. Checked the dates on products. It was finally decided that as well as all the other classes that were to be given over the coming months, cooking was going to be on the list too.

Then there was the basic issue of hunger. People were hungry even with the efforts made. There just never seemed to be enough food. John made weekly trips to the village and to markets, something he was hoping to cut back on as soon as he could before money started to run out. They would eventually start turning out their own fruit and vegetables which had been planted some time before when Ben, Lofty and G had all come down. But John worried about the meat —or lack of it. He needed meat, they all needed meat. They needed the protein, the energy, the iron and even the feel of a steak being cut under a knife with a few bottles of red wine and a green salad. Since arriving at the farm there had been one such meal, served up by John on the first Saturday. That was weeks ago, people would be growing weak and the day would soon be upon them when they could put off the killing of an animal no longer.

But the weather gods were favourable that summer, with long warm evenings and hot days which accelerated growth everywhere, from the tomatoes in the glasshouses to the climbing roses at the front of the house, which took over the trellis and broke out in such great blooms that their scent wafted in through the open windows and filled the rooms with their perfume. The grass was being cut on the lawn two or three times a week and at lunch break they would throw a couple of blankets out there and eat and drink and lather on sun lotion and snooze until after two o'clock, getting tanned and reinvigorated from the sun's rays.

Come early evening John would get the barbecue on and the smell would drift down over the paddock and out the back; he didn't even need to ring the bell to get them in because it was strong. Even if the meat was running out and frozen burgers and lots of roasted vegetables were just being served up, nobody cared. They washed it down with cold lemonade and cider. Music filled the lawn from the open windows of the house. Matt took his guitar down and played. John told stories and Terry told jokes. They stayed in the same clothes all evening, maybe pulling on sweaters closer to nightfall and showered just before bed. Unless it rained, nobody watched TV. They caught the news on the radio over breakfast every morning and left it at that. Newspapers disappeared from the house and John stopped buying them. Phones were switched off most of the day and people checked their emails and networking sites less and less and less. It was starting to look like the perfect summer.

Eleven

The flames from the fire lit the dark of the barnyard in a glow of tawny red, throwing shadows on the walls. Shadows from the bodies, some moving, some dancing, others perched on large round logs the size of truck tyres, the smell of resin still fresh on the wood John had felled that day and chopped into more manageable pieces for the mid-summer bonfire.

G stared into the blaze. The black wood on the edges, the red glow on the outside, the burning embers at the centre. He stared at the shapes made by the flames, like the girls, dancing on the far side of the barn. There in the centre danced an angel with black wings. Then a puppet on a string. Then a couple of lovers intertwined. He watched them and his mind began drifting, brought back suddenly by the intensity of the heat on his outstretched palms.

Butcher was behind him with the jug of poitín.

'You'll go up in smoke if you stay that close.'

He filled G's glass with the sweet, potent liquid, slightly foggy from whatever fruit John had used. He had made gallons last year using the still he had at the back of the barn, a skill he had acquired from his uncle. It wasn't the most pleasant of drinks and the process of making it wasn't too pleasant either and took over six stone of potatoes, six stone of sugar and over a hundred gallons of water, and where his uncle would use turf to provide the heat John just used bottled gas. All the same, the place stank for days. Making cider took even longer and involved pressing hundreds of apples of different varieties and leaving them for weeks to ferment, and it could be very hit and miss. But a batch made in September or October would be ready by June. Mid-summer was when he would sample the new batch and this year, as far as he was concerned, was a good year for both his home brews.

G took a large sip of the poitín, held it, then swallowed hard as tears filled both eyes, chasing it quickly with a swig of cider.

'Jesus Christ, man, I can't do any more of this stuff.'

It was getting late. People were spent from over a month of work but they had needed a break, needed to celebrate something, needed to let off steam and get drunk or stoned or both and allow their bodies to leave their minds alone, if only for one night. So they had chosen the summer solstice and had prepared the traditional bonfire. The night had stayed bright and balmy and warm for as long as it could but fell away exhausted after midnight and blackness rolled in.

Doc was first to drop out, on his way advising people to do likewise as he stumbled over the logs.

'There's a serious hangover in the post, folks. And it'll be here first thing in the morning. Registered. And I'm not signing for it.'

Pete watched him through the gate as he waved without turning.

'He's an oddball, he is. We're here over three weeks and there's hardly been a word out of him.'

Lofty waved back at Doc but he was gone into the darkness.

'Doc's okay. He's had a rough time with stuff the last couple of years, but that's his business. Otherwise, he's okay. Give him a chance.'

Terry was sitting beside Pete and had his head hung down and a glass in both hands.

'What is his background then, Lofty? Do you know anything about him?'

'G knows. He's the one he came to first.' They turned their heads enquiringly in G's direction.

'I don't know much of his background, to be honest. He never told me much. He was away for a year on voluntary work after he got medicine, that's all I know.

When he came back he threw in his career to study Arts. Went off that too and came to us. Can't say why for sure, he's a lot older. Just good to have someone like that around. Anyway, like Lofty said, give him a chance. We all have backgrounds.'

John turned and pulled a log from a pile and lobbed it onto the fire. It rolled into the centre, popped for a moment, then settled.

'He was probably in the killing fields someplace so. Bosnia or Afghanistan or something. Which makes it all the better for us with that experience. What is that music?'

Matt was the only one standing and seemed to be enjoying the music with one leg going at the knee. He looked over to where the girls had brought the stereo out and were dancing loosely on the far side of the yard.

'Some of Joey's eastern stuff. Quite like it myself. Did you hear about the bus herself and Sara were going to organise?'

Ben looked up at him.

'Nothing too far from what we're up to here, Matt.'

'Yeah, but we're in the west of Ireland. They were going to head off to the Middle East via Turkey.'

He plucked a smouldering stick out of the flames and lit a cigarette.

'You have to admire them, but I'm glad they changed their minds. Place is going to go off over there big time.'

All eyes were on the girls. Lofty grinned.

'Why are they dancing like that?'

Hanging low, arms out, breasts up, it was like a limbo only there were no sticks. Though maybe there were in their imagination, as a shout or a scream punctuated the moves.

Terry spat into the fire and caught Joey's eye as she looked over. He waved. But Joey stuck out a tongue and it was followed by a loud laugh and a similar gesture from Jane. Sara had taken Butcher by the hand and was attempting to show him some steps.

Matt smirked and blew a plume over his head.

'So whose idea was it to pick only three girls? Weren't really doing the sums there, were we?'

Terry shuffled out of the way to allow Matt in closer to the heat.

'Sure one of them is taken. Or is she, G?'

'We were all picked for different qualities. Let's say we picked each other. Anyway, there will be more coming. Plenty more when this works out.'

Terry eyed him but said nothing else.

Matt suddenly pulled a silver box from the pocket of his jacket.

'Ah! Who's for a smoke?'

Ben scowled on the other side of the fire.

'What's in that?'

'This is my magic box.'

'But what's in it?'

'Magic.'

He pulled out a packet of cigarette papers curled at the corners and a lump the size of a large grape wrapped in a piece of foil. He burned and rolled and licked and had a produced a joint the size of a 38 ring gauge cigar so fast it was like he pulled it out of the ground.

'Who's for a smoke?'

He lit the joint with an ember burning on the end of a stick and Ben shook his head and reached for a bottle of cider.

'Hate that stuff. We'll be talking shit the whole night after it.'

Matt blew more smoke out than seemed to go in then he coughed from somewhere deep down in his belly.

'Isn't that what we came here to do?'

Terry looked at him in disbelief.

'Are you going to smoke all that? You've been popping shit all night.'

'Had a few stones in the pockets all right.'

G smiled and stared at the end the joint, burning one end smoking at the other.

'I'll have to pass. Last time I smoked skunk I was afraid of people for a week. Caused a psychosis or something. Don't want to be stuck inside some nightmare that won't leave me till it decides to all by itself.'

Lofty took the joint from Matt and sucked on it but winced.

'Has nobody got anything else? Have you got anything else, Matt?'

'Had, sorry. All gone.'

Terry took it next.

'He gave it to the girls. Look at the state of them now. Butcher too. He's on something. The girls all bloody love him.'

Matt took his joint back.

'I saw a film once where this guy fancied a mannequin.'

John looked over at him.

'That was *Lady in Red*.'

'T'wasn't. This was a mannequin. This was a mannequin in a clothes shop and the guy broke in and stole it eventually.'

'I meant the name of the film was *Lady in Red*.'

'Wasn't.'

John turned his eyes to the heavens.

'So what about it then?'

'Well nothing, really, just thinkin' of the need to distinguish lust and desire from a real relationship. Did someone ask that question?'

John shook his head.

'No.'

'Well, I'm asking it then. It could all end badly here what with the terrible gender imbalance. I suggest you do something about that before worrying about where your next steak is going to come from, John. Christ, I'm stoned as Christmas.'

'So what happened in the film?'

'Well he threw her out in the end. Discovered she'd no vagina. I seriously have to go for a walk.'

John laughed, shaking his head.

Matt stood using a large log that needed one or two more chops with an axe as leverage, then guided himself through the gate and out into shadows that enveloped the barnyard.

Ben stared after him.

'Christ. So much for debates and intelligent conversation with the group.'

Pete went to stand up but Terry pulled him back.

'He'll be fine, Pete. He's a big boy.'

Lofty took off his glasses, peered through them, wiped them, then peered through them again.

'We're going to have to clamp down on that shit. We can't afford to have drugs around the place. Making that brew is one thing. Can't risk all those drugs.'

He shook his head and blinked his eyes rapidly as the music was suddenly stopped and Jane and Joey and Sara came over to join them. Butcher refilled everyone's beakers.

A star shot across the sky and all present raised their heads. It left a trail, a white thread which curled then vanished like powder. Joey kept looking skywards while everyone else had bowed and were sitting at the fire watching the embers soften and fall apart.

'Someone make a wish,' she said dreamily.

Sara rearranged a bag half-full of wood shavings into a pillow-like shape and laid her head.

'You already got your wish, Joey.'

'What was that?'

'Coming here.'

'That wasn't my wish.'

Jane moved closer to G and put her head on his shoulder, stretching her arms out to the heat.

'What was your wish then, Joey?'

Joey pulled her knees up under her chin and stared at the flames.

'I wish I had been born ten, twenty, thirty years ago. I feel cheated. Look at the heroes my parents had. Even my older brother. He talks about growing up in the nineties and the music and the ecstasy and the clubs... and he had a great job the whole time too and managed to get a lovely home going. What does our generation have except brands and more brands and dummies in shop windows? We've no heroes. Nobody is around long enough anymore to become a hero. We've no jobs. We've no homes. We've got nothing. This country is going to burn, do you know that? It will start on the high streets in the cities and I can't wait to be sitting up here watching.'

Come four o'clock people slept where they found themselves as the fire retreated into a grey circle. Jane and Joey together on blankets John had pulled from the barn, nobody caring how long they had been in there or what other animal had used it for warmth so long as they had the warmth too. Jackets, sweaters and sack cloth rolled out on nothing but the ground that had steamed and dried out. Nobody wanted to leave that afterglow or turn their backs on the night they had lost themselves in, but surrender to the dark instead and go with it into morning.

But from somewhere out there in the pitch where no eyes could see there came a sound that was not startling enough to awaken them immediately, but unsettling enough in its depth and tone to cause a disturbance in the minds of those that slept together. Jane jumped first just as the echoes waned around the walls of the yard.

'What was that?'

G raised his head then hugged it.

'Don't know. Jesus.'

'Where's Matt? G?'

'He went off a while ago. He was out of it.'

Jane turned behind her and looked, but only as far as the dark would allow.

'Well, what was that noise?'

'I don't know, Jane, we're on a farm. Relax.'

Bodies rose from the ground in slow motion. Joey was the first to climb to her feet, wrapping her long blonde mane in an elastic removed from her wrist.

'I heard something too, Jane. What was it, John?'

'Pig. Fox. Owl. Rat. Take your pick.'

'Well, it's creepy. I bet somebody's watching us right now.'

'Don't be stupid, there's nobody within miles of this place.'

G took Jane's hand and helped her stand.

'Let's all just get to bed. I'll stay here and shovel clay on the fire. John and Lofty help everyone else inside.'

A large shovel with a mouth like a dead pike was propped against the wall in the barn, finding a groove in the corrugated iron to settle in. G took it and slung it over his shoulder, balancing the weight of the metal as he heard the retreat up the gravel path, the squeak of the gate, the rattle of the back door, and the last of the voices trail away.

It was deathly still and quiet save the odd pop from the coals and G stopped at the warm ashes, leaning hard on the wooden handle of the shovel with a metal 'T' top. His head was spinning from strong alcohol and he stumbled out to the edge of the yard to dig up some clay, catching sight of the enormity of the surrounding farm and the tiny shell of light they had been huddled around all night.

A chill had fallen and G hurried back and forward to the embers with the shovel of clay picking up pace each time. On the edge of darkness he dug hard into the ground, the metal grating on the stony soil like a gravedigger's spade. The earth grew damp and the smell was of decay. Blackness bore down on his shoulders. With the fire dead there lay nothing but a mound of clay smoking as if a crack had formed in the earth and no light was left either. He paused and stood over it but felt the emptiness all around. Then he let the shovel drop where he stood and moved quickly up the path towards the light shining from the farmhouse windows.

Twelve

Light pierced the pattern on the net curtains over Lofty's window and stabbed at his eyes. He rubbed it away but it insisted so he sat up and hung his head and shielded himself with his hand. It was early but not too early and the house was quiet and already starting to warm up. He got up and tiptoed down the corridor, pulling a sweater over his head as he walked and slowly opened the door to G's room.

G was sprawled across the bed from left to right, his arms dangling over the edge and almost reaching the floor where a pint glass full of water was within easy reach when he needed it. Lofty called him in a voice just above a whisper, more of a croak, and G stirred but didn't move. When Lofty called him again he lifted his head slowly as if it were on old hinges.

'What time's it, Lofty?'

'Quarter to nine.'

'Holy Jesus.'

'G, get up. There are lots and lots of things to do.'

'Oh Lofty, thank God you woke me.'

G pulled himself up and looked under the duvet.

'I had such a nightmare. There was a scarecrow. Spiders. Spiders under my duvet. A huge fire and smoke. And that shed at the bottom of the paddock. Such an awful nightmare, Lofty.'

'Precisely all the things you saw yesterday. Except the scarecrow maybe. Memories, not nightmares, old boy. I wouldn't worry about it. You probably only had it five minutes ago. Now get your arse up.'

'No, it was different than that. God, Lofty. I swear I think somebody might have been murdered in this room. I have to talk to John. Just go down quickly and get me some painkillers, Lofty. I don't care what they are, just something for this pain before I get up.'

Lofty smiled, crept downstairs to the kitchen and went through the cupboards coming back with two tablets which he put into G's mouth, lifting the water up for him to wash them down.

'Ten minutes, G. Downstairs.'

When G finally crawled into the kitchen Lofty had tea steaming in a pot and, bread freshly toasted and yoghurt on the table.

'Will you have something to eat, G? It'll do you good.'

'God no, just a cup of tea. Maybe toast. Whatever you gave me is working on my head, but it's the rest of me...'

G sat down and gripped the tea tightly in both hands, wincing slowly every time he sipped from it. Then he took a piece of toast and broke off a crust to chew on.

'What is it, Lofty? Why are you looking at me like that?'

Lofty pulled off his glasses.

'I've bad news, G.'

'Oh no, I don't want to hear it Lofty, tell someone else.'

'Matt never went to bed. I just went in to wake him and he's not there.'

'What do you mean he's not there?'

'I mean he's not there, old boy. Gone, I suppose. Or never came back.'

G finished his toast slowly and sipped his tea. Lofty leaned over and took the yoghurt.

'Do you mind?'

G looked at Lofty as he removed the lid from the yoghurt and licked it.

'No. We better go and look for him, Lofty. Maybe he's packed it in, never trusted him anyway. Has to be a first dropout. Or maybe he just fell asleep somewhere. I know he wandered off after he had his smoke. Probably just shacked up with one of the girls for God's sake.'

It was warm when they got outside and by the time they had got to the barnyard a group of flies that hadn't yet formed a swarm had picked up on the sweat, laden with alcohol. G swatted over his head and sweated more as he did so, and for the first time cursed the countryside which he had begun to call home.

There was nobody in the barnyard, just a pile of smouldering ashes, a large collection of receptacles and beakers, some still full of the liquor they had consumed the previous night, and the shovel sticking out of the ground like a marker.

'Should have put that away. John hates leaving his gear outside.'

'It's not gear it's just a shovel and it was darker than hell here last night, believe it or not.'

'Okay, we'll split up, G. I'll head across the paddock to the river and you check around the buildings. Could be crashed in the outhouses someplace.'

When Lofty had disappeared up to his waist in the long grass G went over and sat down on a log near the mound of ash that was still warm. He wretched suddenly from somewhere deep, in a part of his belly he couldn't even name, and spat a string of green bile which sizzled and popped like a lump of fat, then wiped his mouth with the sleeve of his shirt.

Out across the paddock a breeze was bending stripes in the grass downwards towards the river like a shoal of fish and in the middle was Lofty wading through, his arms out for balance. How beautiful it looked compared to the scene only hours before when nothing could have penetrated the darkness and a thousand things could have been moving around within it and G wouldn't have known.

Suddenly Lofty stopped, balanced on one leg as if he had stumbled on something, then he waved frantically calling G over to where he stood. G got up and broke into a trot, straight away feeling the hard clay floor of the barnyard give way to the soft grass of the paddock which slowed him down and forced him to raise his knees up to his chest as he ran.

'What is it, Lofty?'

Lofty didn't answer only stared at the ground in front of him waving at G the whole time.

G was out of breath and weak at the knees when he got to where Lofty was standing gazing down at the body of Matt, which lay spread on the grass in a crooked 'X'.

There was a smell from where he lay and his cap had fallen off to reveal a balding patch on the top of his head. His mouth hung open, and every insect from ant to horsefly was crawling in or around it and the ones above G's head which had now become a swarm joined in too.

'At least we know why he wears that cap all the time now.'

Lofty stared at him in disbelief.

'G, he could be in trouble.'

'He's fine.'

Lofty tried to wake him, slapping his face a bit, but Matt didn't stir. So he pulled off his sweater, lifted Matt's head to raise it from the damp grass and wedged it underneath, suddenly noticing a blotch of dried blood the colour of black grape beneath it.

'He's bleeding. Or he was. Look.'

'Get Doc, Lofty, quick.'

Lofty charged off into the grass while G got down beside Matt and put his ear to his chest, hearing a gentle wheeze from somewhere inside.

'Matt. Matt. Can you hear me?'

G sighed and stood back up staring at the bright green grass with the red stain from Matt's blood which had dried where it entered the earth.

'Matt, you're going to be okay. Do you hear me?'

Matt let out a sigh, or maybe it was just air but G took it for an answer.

'The doc is coming soon, don't you worry.'

Behind him across the paddock came Matt and Doc who looked considerably fresh and was in the lead and walking fast. He said nothing when he saw Matt, just got down on his knees and peeled back an eyelid.

'What happened him?'

G stole a glance at Lofty who had arrived out of breath and gripping his side. He shrugged.

'Any drugs?'

'He had pills that he was passing out. And the skunk he had rolled up. That's what did it, I think.'

Doc sighed loudly and bent down further to examine Matt, the pupils of his eyes ringed by yellow circles. There was a groan from Matt followed by a raised arm pushing Doc's hand away.

'At least he's still in the land of the living.'

He turned Matt's head over and saw the wound in the scalp.

'He's got a gash here. It looks like someone has whacked him on the head.'

Doc pointed to a crescent-shaped cut at the back of Matt's head just above the neck where the blood had clotted and his hair had clumped like wet straw.

'I'd like to get him to a hospital just in case. He might have been concussed from this.'

'No way, Doc. No hospitals, not now.'

'G, anyone who has suffered concussion has to be taken for observation.'

'Sorry Doc, first thing they'll do is a blood test and he's full of drugs. It could drag us into a world of shit and close this thing down. You observe him, that's why you're here. If he hasn't come round by this afternoon then we'll talk as a group. Anyway, he probably just fell.'

'Fell on what, G? There's nothing here but grass.'

G looked around him at the likely path Matt would have taken from the barnyard across the paddock and the likely obstacles in the way. There were none.

'All right, we better get him upstairs and I'll check him out further. I'm waiting two hours, G, if he hasn't come round by then we're going. That's it. And I need you to go down the town and get some materials in the pharmacy. Can you do that?'

'Sure, we'll go.'

They lifted Matt up and carried him into the house taking it in turns at either end while one guided and watched for uneven ground. The house had shook itself out of sleep; showers ran, kettles boiled, upstairs someone had turned their stereo on, and the clock in the hall chimed ten times. There was enough noise to cover the sound of Matt being dragged up the steps, groaning, to his room. G left him, thankful that nobody had seen them as they came in and he went then to John's room at the furthest end of the corridor.

He knocked but didn't wait for a reply and entered quickly. John was shaving over the small sink in the corner of his room, shaking the blade into a pool of suddy water. He wore nothing but jeans and his belly rippled with the slightest of movements.

'Nice morning, G.'

'Looks like it.'

John rinsed the blade and took up a small pair of scissors and clipped at his eyebrows.

'Sleep okay?'

'No. Awful sleep.'

'Well, I warned you all about the homemade brew.'

He threw water over his face then dried it vigorously with a towel turning the skin a deeper hue of red than it normally was.

'John, we found Matt outside in the paddock this morning. Slept there all night.'

'Jesus. Is he okay?' He looked alarmed.

'He's a cut on the back of his head. Doc says someone hit him.'

John began dressing, his head half way up his jumper. He popped out and stared at G.

'Hit him?'

'That's what Doc said. Didn't look like it to me.'

'Sure Jesus, G, he fell or something.'

'That's what I said.'

'Fuck it. We've survived so far. Tell Doc not to go mouthing off about him getting hit though. Could do without that shit.'

G left John and went down the stairs hearing two people arguing loudly below, drowning the music that came from one of the bedrooms.

'Can we not have a day off, man?'

'Terry, we can't. Especially not you.'

'Why not? It's been over a month.'

G entered the living room where Ben stood at arm's length from Terry.

'Let me put you in the picture. It'll be autumn before you know it.'

'It's only the end of June!'

'We're going to need those outhouses done soon. We're still behind in here. We also want to finish planting this week, and there's tomatoes falling off the bloody plants in the glasshouses. If we don't stay on top, we lose control. Have you got that? If we get out and move we'll have the hangover's sweated out by midday.'

'Well that's really something to look forward to.'

'You're without Matt as well, guys.'

Ben spun on G.

'What's that?'

'Matt's out for lunch.'

Terry smirked and sat down on the couch to join Pete. He picked up a mug of tea and took a piece of French toast from a large pile on a plate in the centre of the coffee table.

'Ah, he's not much use anyway, God love him.'

On a chair under the large bay window Joey was eating fruit chopped in a bowl.

'What happened him?'

'Well, he's just rough after last night. He'll be fine though.'

'We're all rough, G.'

'Well he's rougher.'

Pete shook his head.

'So Matt gets a day in bed and the rest of us have to work. That's great that is.'

'Sorry guys. He is actually in a bad way. And if he doesn't get better we'll have to bring him to hospital.'

Terry laughed.

'Better off leaving him here.'

'Well, anyway. I'm going down the town with Lofty to get some medical supplies. Anyone need anything.'

'So you're going down the town? With Lofty I suppose? And the rest of us... can sweat until midday.'

G sighed and looked at his watch.

'Jesus, Terry. I'll be an hour. Anyone else need anything while I'm down there? Any other problems.'

'There are spiders in my room, G.'

G sat on Lofty's rocking chair and rubbed his eyes as he rocked back as far as the chair would go then tilted there dangerously for a moment.

'Well they're only small fuckers, Jane.'

'But small fuckers grow into big fuckers, G. It just looks like there could be a nest or something. Can you get something in the hardware or something? There's a lot of ants out the back at the kitchen door too.'

Butcher raised a hand and G rocked forward again.

'There's no need to raise your hand, Butcher. This is not official, we're just talking.'

'Toilet's blocked on the top floor.'

'Terry, that's you're department.'

'No way, mate. That John was in there this morning, he can look after that.'

'Well, someone fix the thing. Anything else?'

'What about getting extra lights outside?'

'We have lights outside, Sara.'

'Not at the back. It was pitch dark coming in from the fire last night and we could hardly see a thing. I fell, actually.'

Sara lifted her right leg and crossed it over her left then rolled her jeans up to her knee to reveal a bruise that was marbled blue and black just half-way up her shin. She prodded it delicately with her finger and winced.

'Bloody sore, so it is.'

'We all fell coming in last night, we were all pissed.'

'I didn't drink that much, G.'

'Well, whatever you girls were on then that you didn't bother to share with the rest of us. We'll get a light out the back. It is dark, I agree. Can I go now?'

'There is one more thing.'

'What's that Joey?'

'You and John out shooting all the time.'

'It's not all the time.'

'A lot of the time.'

'Some of the time. What's the problem with it? We hunt. Shoot crows.'

'Exactly, there's dead crows around the place, G. I'm coming across them in the vegetable gardens and it's not hygienic. Do you want me to discuss it with Doc? Bloody things are full of maggots.'

'Well, we're trying to scare them off.'

'That's what scarecrows are for.'

'John doesn't like scarecrows.'

'He's afraid of scarecrows so he trains you to shoot the crows instead? What kind of farm is this? Can the dogs not fetch them or something?'

'They're sheep dogs, not retrievers. Besides, you didn't mind eating pheasant last week.'

'I didn't eat it, I'm vegetarian.'

'Well aren't you blessed that vegetables don't fly. Jesus Joey, is this how the day is going to go?'

'I'm just saying dead animals spread disease. You should know that. John should definitely know that.'

G nodded and stood up and brought his voice down to a whisper as he left.

'I know that, I know that. I'll keep the shooting down, okay Joey. We'll burn the dead crows in future.'

Thirteen

Coming from the city as he did, G had few occasions as a kid to get out into the country. His grandmother lived in the countryside somewhere but G could never remember exactly where it was. All he remembered were the long drives down the coast, then arriving in time for Sunday dinner on the Sundays that he did go with his family, which was about once a month.

The summer trips were bearable because he was let loose out into the garden and over the fence at the back and into the trees where the whole world seemed bigger. Bigger flowers, weeds as big as he was, bigger rocks and stones, and bigger insects in a fantasy world to a small kid.

The winters though were spent locked inside with the older folk around the table then moving into the sitting room gathered at a fire and watching the shapes form. Bright red ones dancing at the top and dark malicious ones that lay under the surface. He used to think that the dark shapes were trying to drag the bright ones down. He figured that in the end they always won because when the fire had gone out all that was left was cold, black dust.

His da used to look forward to those trips regardless of the seasons since it got him out of the housing estate and his ma said it was good therapy to be in the countryside every now and again, that the air was good and the fresh colours would soothe the mind. Not like the drab greys of the estate where even the grass on the greens had an off-yellow pallor. G's da had been ill. It did him no good to have lost the job and the house and have to move into a small estate. But a lot of people in those times, the 1980s, had to do the same thing if they weren't in a position to get out altogether. G's sister left. Took a boat to England. He loved his sister but he hardly ever saw her after that. And he swore that if the bad times ever came around again he wouldn't leave, because it tears people apart.

One summer G and his da went into the trees at the back of his grandmother's house with a length of thick rope and a tyre and made a rope swing that flew out over a river and back on to the bank, much better than the one he had made with Mack and Duff behind the football pitch. The only problem was that G would come back with mud on his best trousers because he didn't use his legs properly on the backswing. This would drive his ma mad but his da didn't seem to mind all that much.

But one afternoon, when G was there swinging out over the river and back again in an arc for what seemed like hours, he noticed a small bird fall from the sky and land on the soft grass at the bank of the river. It was wounded but not dead. It looked like it had been attacked or had been thrown from its nest. So he took it back to his grandmother's house cupped in his hands to keep it warm and safe and to stop it from flapping about and falling all over again.

When his grandmother saw it she said there was little they could do because if you took something from the wild and tried to make it live somewhere else it would die. Things can't live in another environment, you just can't force nature, it doesn't work like that, she said. The bird had been attacked, she told him, probably by crows. Crows were bad, came from hell and acted as the devil's eyes during the day because he didn't like the daytime, only the night. The birds were angels, so you should never kill the birds, only the crows. G's grandmother even kept several metal traps at the back of her house, large wire cages that caught both crows and magpies. The cage had three compartments, one wide enough to keep a live bird in that acted as a decoy, the other two had spring doors and a split perch. Once a bird was attracted into one of these compartments it would land on the perch and the perch would drop under the weight of the bird to ensnare it in the cage. G's grandmother caught birds every day, mostly crows and magpies. She would then kill them with a hammer, which G found frightening the first time he saw it done. When a new bird was captured, it would replace the decoy bird who would be killed. But eventually G was able to kill some of the crows himself after his grandmother had told him tales about how evil they all were.

So the day G found the bird, he went up on to the roof of his grandmother's house and threw it high into the air in a flurry of tiny feathers to make it fly back to its own world. It flapped its wings for a moment looking like a kite about to catch a current, then plummeted to earth like a stone.

G felt really bad. He felt he had killed the bird after his grandmother told him that he should never have taken it away from its own environment. That night he couldn't sleep. He lay there wondering if the crows would follow him for the rest of his days for what he had done. So he decided there and then that crows would have to be killed whenever they got too close. And when too many got too close, it was surely a bad omen.

Fourteen

G had expected all the smells of the rural town to be there as John had described them that first day when he had taken G down in his car to his farm. The bakery, the butcher, the fish shop, strong tea from the local café and chips on newspaper drowned in vinegar. But it didn't seem that way as he and Lofty walked through the main street that afternoon.

'Are you hungry, Lofty?'

'Bit, yeah.'

'Well, what do you fancy? Think for a minute and tell us what would go down well now after last night.'

'I suppose a strong coffee. Pastry maybe.'

'Oh Jesus, Lofty. We're going to get a fry, and we're going to enjoy it.'

They walked on up the main street past a small bookshop that had closed its doors with a 'To Let' sign pointed downwards from the first floor. A butcher's shop was closed too, windows whitewashed, and in the doorway an assortment of paper, dirt and empty cans had blown into the corners. A pub at one end of the main street looked desolate. In the alley next to it was a skip. G peered over the edge at broken stools and taps and cracked crates, so maybe it hadn't closed up that long. There was a light on inside too and two workers were dismantling the bar.

'We could use that bar, you know.'

'Do you want to go and ask them, G. I'm sure they could use the money.'

'Do you have any?'

'Twenty quid.'

'Won't get you the bar. Won't help them much either.'

They passed a fruit and veg store in the shadow of a supermarket and a cash for gold store where there was once a coffee house. Over the bridge the only remaining bank had a notice it was closing and taking its business to another town. The hardware store was moving to an industrial estate off the main road and was being joined by the car dealer section of the garage, but the petrol pumps were remaining.

'Matt was right, Lofty. It's happening all over.'

They reached the end of the main street and gazed across the field at a housing estate that looked as if it had toppled out of a toy chest. Some homes were finished, others were halfway there. Some homes had cars in the front and a lawn and a flower bed in full bloom, others had abandoned mortar mixers and patches of clay.

Kids ran around playing with piping and electric cable, making bridges across gullies with planks of wood. Puddles formed in the middle of roadways where one kid floated a toy boat.

'Fuck this, Lofty. Better off up at the farm.'

'Will we get that fry do you think?'

The door to the cafe was wedged open with a bit of timber and two young girls were behind a counter making up sandwiches from stainless steel containers full of sticky coleslaw, chopped vegetables and sliced meats and cheeses. One of the girls came down into the dining area with a cloth and wiped a table, leaving a streak that smelled of pee.

'Can I get you something?'

She had an accent that was not native.

'Well, we were looking some breakfast.'

The girl looked over at the board where the word 'special' was written in the singular above a list of things that weren't very special and shook her head.

'We finished breakfast I'm afraid. We have lasagne and chips, paninis, toasted cheese and ham… '

G looked at Lofty then up at the girl.

'Where are you from?'

'I'm from Slovakia.'

'Lucky you. How long have you been here?'

'Two years. But I'm going home next month. I have a new job.'

She smiled and her face smiled with it.

'Lucky you again. We'll just have two coffees, Americanos, large. And two pastries.'

'That's it?'

'That's it.'

The coffee grinder crunched behind them then hissed and spat and the girl came back with two soup bowls of coffee on a tray with two pastries.

'There you are. Enjoy.'

G tore three sugar parcels open with his teeth and poured them into the coffee, added milk and stirred the lot with a spoon until the coffee tipped over on to the saucer then he licked the spoon clean and dropped it with a metallic clang.

'So much for the big breakfast.'

'You're the one that wanted to come down here. And you better come back with all the goods or the others will kill you.'

'Sure. Don't let me forget some insecticide in the hardware, will you?'

'Hardware is closed.'

'Closing. Relocating it says actually. We'll buy some wine, few bottles of red'll keep them all happy.'

Lofty bit into his pastry and spat flakes as he went to talk.

'G, have you thought about who is serious and who isn't in all of this?'

'Course I have. You?'

'Sure.'

'Well I'll give you my names and you say yay or nay. John, Joey and Sara, Butcher, maybe Doc and… I'd say that's it.'

'Right. And Terry.'

'Good bloke. But don't know. I've a feeling him and his mate Pete might get fed up.'

'Well, get rid of them then before they do.'

'They're getting a load of work done. We'll hang on to them as long as we can. What do you think Ben will do?'

'Hate to see him go, G. But he is going to go. You know that. He's had his eye on Australia for a while now. They're putting packages together over there now. Good offers.'

'Yeah. He's gone. He gave it a shot though. Kept his word.'

'Jane?'

G shook his head.

'I don't know. I wish she wasn't here, to be honest.'

'Why is she here then?'

'Well, she was part of it all along, Lofty. We used to talk about it, plan it. When we finished up, we agreed she could come down. I couldn't just leave her out.'

'So she's well over you then? I mean, if she was able to come down and be that close, without being close.'

G shrugged and tapped the top of his pastry with his spoon.

'Sorry, old boy. See you still have something for her. Plenty more fish and all that.'

'No, it's not like that. I just wonder whether this thing is going to suit her. I should really tell her to go, but at the same time we were together so long part of me doesn't want to see her leave.'

'Can't offer counsel on any of that. But I would say to go easy on Joey?'

'Joey?'

'She gets it when you're giving it out.'

'She can be a pain in the arse, that girl.'

'Just conflict, G. We spoke about this. And you going round shooting things with John all the time. What was that shit with the crows, for Christ's sake?'

'She's nuts about animals. I can't for the life of me figure out what she came here for. I mean, what did she think we were going to be doing?'

'But *I'm* even starting to wonder what all this target practice on crows and shit is all about.'

'Maybe we were careless. She's right about that. We have a few traps behind the barn too for the little bastards. My grandmother showed me how to make them.'

Lofty shook his head.

'What the hell have you got against crows? Jesus, we've enough worries up there.'

'You wouldn't understand.'

'No, I probably wouldn't. Traps? Jesus, G. You know something like that will freak those girls out.'

'Ah Lofty, for God's sake. I mean just wait until we have to get one of those pigs. Then a cow maybe. No faces on steaks, you know.'

'That's John's line.'

'Well, we should be repeating it then.'

When they returned they were greeted by John who was cutting the lawn on his ride-on at the front of the house, moving in large circles and spitting out cuttings to one side each time he turned. Behind him there was a trail of spent smoke, grey and putrid from the two-stroke engine which at least kept the flies at bay.

When he saw Lofty and G approach he stopped the mower and climbed down, slapping the cuttings from his thighs and shoulders.

'You can grab a rake there if you like, G, do some work.'

G looked at the cut grass which had formed into damp clumps.

'Sure, I'll go and get changed. Any word on Matt?'

'He's moving. He'll live. Fuckin eejit.'

G went inside through the back door and found Doc in the kitchen with a pot of tea at his elbow, sitting in the alcove at the table scribbling on sheets of paper with several books piled in front of him. He had his glasses on and one hand under his chin and didn't even look up when G came in.

'Okay there, Doc?'

'Fine, yeah.'

'How's Matt doing?'

'He's fine. Did you get the stuff I asked for?'

G held up the paper bag.

'What are you up to there, Doc?'

Doc looked up slowly and stared at G who had poured a glass of water and was standing over the table sipping it.

'Making some notes. I'd like to give that talk tomorrow evening if I may. I'm about, what, six weeks late already. Apologies for that. I was busy helping out.'

G shrugged and tried to peer over into Doc's work.

'Great. So what's it all about?'

'What's it all about? Well, in no particular order, general health and well-being, nutrition, safety and use of equipment, chemicals that we're going to come into contact with, cleanliness and hygiene in the kitchens – they're like shit sometimes depending on who is on the roster, not you G, by the way – cleanliness and hygiene in the bathrooms, cleanliness around the farm, cleanliness around the house. Even basic stuff like washing hands properly, G. Alcohol poisoning…'

Doc stopped for a moment and tapped his pen as he looked up at G and pointed to the paper bag he had in his hand.

'Types of disease that can be picked up from animals like rats, sheep, pigs, all the rest. How to handle livestock. The dangers of leaving raw meat with cooked meat in refrigerators —which I happen to have seen just right here today and we all could have been sick. Dangers of leaving animal carcasses around untreated.'

Doc looked up again over the top of his glasses.

'That includes dead birds, G. I heard about that. Joey told me. You can't be leaving dead birds in places where there are people working manually. Are you stupid? How to store our food for the long term. How to season and preserve meats properly. Danger from insects. Avoiding parasites. That includes things you can pick up from the grass, G.'

Doc smiled this time as he looked up. But it vanished quickly.

'I've seen you chewing grass. I wouldn't do that if I were you. Especially when we invest in more cows. Farmyard safety. Chainsaw accidents. Accidents with knives, hand tools and axes and stuff. Back pain and how to lift heavy objects properly. Cuts, lacerations, bruises, sprains, breaks and how to administer proper first aid and recovery. As you can see, I've been taking note of the things we'll have to sort out if we're to stay here without a serious fuck-up. And I mean a serious fuck up. Not one of Matt's silly episodes. That's a different matter.'

'Thought you said that was serious.'

'No, no. I never said that. It was stupid though. And that's about it so far. But I'll keep working.'

Doc put his glasses back on and continued writing.

'Okay. Sounds like you've covered it all there, Doc. But can I ask you something? Put the pen down for a minute will you?'

Doc dropped the pen.

'I've never really asked you about why you wanted to come down here. I mean, really asked you.'

'I thought we agreed that I could at least keep those personal feelings to myself. I'm working as hard as anyone else here.'

G pulled out a chair and sat down with the back rest out in front.

'It's not about the work, Doc. You know we're supposed to be a group here. The others are asking about you Doc, you know what I mean?'

'There are some as quiet as myself.'

'But they're quiet by nature, Doc. You're not. I know you're not. Anyway, they mix a bit more. I know it's only early days yet, but it's not good.'

Doc took off his glasses and put them down slowly on the table. He ran his hands through his hair which was longer at the front than at the back and sides and sighed loudly.

'We all have a story G, don't we? I worked hard in college, school. I wanted to study medicine because I thought it was my vocation, not for myself but for others. You know. That's why most of us go into it, as a vocation. Save lives, save the world. All that.'

'And what about it?'

'Well it's not worth saving, is it?'

G couldn't avoid breaking into a laugh.

'There's nothing amusing about it, G. Actually it's quite tragic coming from someone with a medical qualification.'

'Sorry. I suppose you don't get many people coming out with statements like that. I mean, you are a bit young for it.'

'I'm the oldest here, G. By a bit too. And let's just say I've seen more than you have. Or anyone else here for that matter.'

'Where?'

'I'm not going to talk about it, G. You've asked me that already, now please don't ask me again.'

'Okay. But you've never given me an answer to the question of your wanting to come here, Doc. We deserve that at least. So why here? What do you hope for here? I mean you are one of the few actually qualified people here. The rest of us will just have basic degrees.'

'Okay, well believe it or not I came here first and foremost for some peace. I did my homework on places like this, G, when I heard about it. Although this is starting to look more like a different model. I thought it was mad to begin with but then I realised how many similar places like this exist all over the world. It really fascinated me. And the more I thought about it, the more sense it made. You find the world too vast, too scary, too unpredictable. You make your own. It's like a shell, isn't it? Particularly now the way things are. And it's going to get a hell of a lot worse, G. Do you realise that?'

G swirled the water around in his glass and looked at the bottom.

'I'm starting to realise there might be a long way to go before things get better.'

'Right. But you've no idea what real poverty is like, G. What can happen. What it can do to people. I've seen it. If this thing works, it could very well be a stroke of genius. People have been living in their own communities for hundreds of years, independently, proper functioning communities, G. I never figured it. I mean, long term, I don't know if this place can sustain it. We'll see. But, to answer your question finally, if I can help a group of people here, who think like me and who want to live like me, then that is my vocation. Do you get it? But not out there. And certainly not in this State with the way the health system is. Here. I want this to work. That's all.'

Doc put his glasses back on and got back to his work so G stood up and went to walk out, turning suddenly as he reached the door.

'Tell me something, Doc. How far would you go to keep this thing alive? I mean, really.'

'What do you mean exactly?'

'I don't really know, Doc. Just, things like this take more than physical work, don't they? They take resolve and mental will to keep convincing yourself every day that it can work. We have to keep that in our heads, Doc. We have to protect it. You know.'

Doc stared at G for a moment.

'Sure, G. Sure, I know. Protect it. You're right.'

Fifteen

You'll protect me. That's what Jane had said to G so many times when they were together. You'll protect me. From what? G had asked. She didn't know. But she said that love was about protection. So G asked her who was going to protect him. And she didn't know either. A guardian angel perhaps. That was her guess. And G had got to wonder if there might have been any kind of sense in that. That in order for him to protect her he would need guidance from something else.

He remembered having to protect his first girlfriend, if he could call her a girlfriend. They were so young, only kids. But they became close, as young as they were. It was about a year after the incident in school, when G and his family had moved to another part of the city when the bottom had fallen out of his dad's world. It was a part of the city they'd never imagined going to. G remembered the day well. It was in the month of November and it was cold and damp and there was even a sense of snow in the air.

They drove in through the estate, his ma, da and sister, staring at the small houses, half of which were boarded up and vacant and covered in graffiti, and out past the windswept playing fields with a scorched circle from a bonfire in the centre. G's da stopped the car to take a look over the fields at the mountains that formed a ring around the city and remarked that maybe it wasn't as bad as all that, and G took in the bonfire area, the scorch still fresh from when it had burned at Halloween. It must have been stacked high before it was lit. Stacked with anything that people could get their hands on. There was even the shell of a mattress on the ground, the springs blackened and lifeless and beside it the entrails of several tyres. It seemed people would burn just about anything at all on Halloween.

The first night, G sat in his room alone. He lay on the bed and stared at the opposite wall where strips of wallpaper had been torn off by the previous child. He wondered who it was. A boy or a girl. Where were they now and why had they left. Had they moved up in the world or slipped further down. The whole house had been completely empty when they'd arrived, with only the things that people want to leave behind laying on the floors. But of all those things there was nothing to betray what kind of family had lived there and where they had gone to.

Then G suddenly heard a noise outside on the street below, like a whipping sound. A rope. Someone was skipping. He listened carefully and could hear in between the slash of the rope striking the tarmac the sound of a girl singing.

He sat up quickly and climbed onto the desk at the window, opened it, put his elbows on the sill and looked out. There on the street, all alone, was a young girl skipping and singing to herself. G stared at her. She was pretty. And she was reciting some skipping rhyme he'd never heard before. So he listened for some time until she suddenly stopped and looked up. Then she put the down the rope.

'What are you staring at?'

G shrugged. He wanted to climb back down onto his bed. He'd never heard a girl speak like that before, so bold and so brazen.

'What are you staring at?'

'I wasn't staring I was just listening.'

'Well don't listen.'

Then she picked up the rope and turned and raised two fingers at G before skipping away once more, only this time moving as she skipped and went into a house further down the street.

G had met Jane the first year in University at an evening guest lecture. He had spotted her sitting a few rows further down from where he sat. A couple of times when she looked around he caught her eye, but before the lecture finished she turned around and looked directly at him. So when the lecture ended he stood quickly and followed her as the crowds left, finally catching up with her at the main doors of the building. He stopped her and simply asked her to go with him for a coffee or a beer. She took her time answering. Stared at him for a few moments, looked around, then back at him, keeping him waiting to see how long he could stand there.

'Okay, I'll go for a beer.'

They were inseparable for almost the duration of their term in college and remained close until the final year when pressures began to drive them apart. G knew that it was not what either of them wanted but it was how shit from the outside can divide a perfectly good relationship from the inside and tear it all apart.

'Enjoying a stroll?'

G stopped and turned. Jane was there on one of the benches that John had put at various places around the farm for people to chill out on, good solid benches made of all-natural cedar that would weather well and last many winters. He had made them with Terry over the last few weeks without telling anyone where he had put them, so people could wander off on their own in the evenings and find a bench near the woods or down at the river or even over the hill in the far field that lay fallow that year and was a great tangle of grass and weeds and tall flowers.

G pretended to squint against the light of a sun that was almost gone. Jane smiled and pulled out a packet of cigarettes, handing one to G as he sat and for a couple of minutes neither spoke, just smoked the cigarettes and soaked up the silence.

'So how do you feel about everything so far, G? Happy?'

'Good. And you?'

'Honestly?'

Jane blew a column of smoke up over her head and looked across at the river.

'I'm happy I came here, G. Really. It's like I've taken my head to a laundrette and cleaned out all the shit that's been stuck spinning inside it for years. Will it last though?'

'Why wouldn't it?'

Jane shrugged and flicked her cigarette onto the ground, stamping it down with the heel of her boot.

'What's the matter? I know that look, Jane. What is it?'

'It's not a big deal yet but it soon will be if we don't sort it out.'

'What's that?'

'Money, I'm afraid. You put me in charge of the accounts and John's files and haven't given me the chance to talk to you about any of it yet. Any time I've tried you've been too busy. We're pretty broke, you know.'

'How broke?'

'It's not just the group finances. We can stretch that out for a while and we're not starving. But there are other things, G. There are bills coming in all the time. Electricity, gas, TV and broadband, day-to-day shopping and supplies, people just ordering stuff at random... then there's the payments on this farm.'

'Payments on this farm?'

'See. This is exactly what I'm talking about, G. You haven't a clue. John's uncle left him with a lot of debts.'

'I knew that.'

'Yeah? Well he consolidated his debts and re-mortgaged with the bank to pay them off. Most of them. Now he owes the bank. And he hasn't been meeting his monthly payments.'

'Since when?'

'He's behind five months now. The letters are coming in and they're not nice.'

'Jesus, why does John keep all these secrets from me? We're supposed to be in this together.'

'He's going to have to go down and talk to the bank. I've mentioned it to him but he's got his head up his ass.'

'I'll go.'

'They won't talk to you, G.'

'They will. They'll talk to anyone about money these days. They need it.'

'But you haven't got it.'

'I'll make them a deal.'

'Using what as barter?'

G looked about him.

'This.'

Jane laughed.

'Well, I don't know what you had in mind, but best of luck. There's one other thing that I can't get to the bottom of.'

'What's that? More money?'

Jane sat forward and put her hands together between her knees.

'No. This is something a bit more sinister, G.'

She took a look over her shoulder and began speaking in a lower voice.

'Did John ever speak to you about a legal case here? Anything to do with the land?'

'Never. I don't like where this is going, Jane.'

'No. You won't.'

Jane looked around again up beyond the far field and into the hills, but dusk was preventing much from being seen.

'From what I can gather from some of the documents, and I'm no legal expert, it looks as if there was some battle or maybe even a deal over land between the Caseys and some guys called the brothers MacMillen. There's a paper trail but it runs out fairly quickly.'

'Are there names of lawyers or anything?'

'No. Just a few fairly crude documents. And there's an address for the brothers, Quarry Road.'

'Where's that?'

Jane waved behind her.

'Looks like it runs up behind the farm somewhere. Look, I'm not snooping any further on this. You can. Or you can ask John. I've enough to be getting on with sorting out the finances.'

'Bastard's been hiding this for a reason. Fair enough. I'll go and snoop.'

'How are you going to manage that?'

'Ask.'

'Right, but when and where?'

'As soon as I can, down the town. I'll tell John I got to head home for a night or two and crash in a bed and breakfast or something. He won't know. I'll dig up as much as I can and throw it back at him. We got to nail stuff like this before we devote any more time and energy to the place. It's not fair on the people.'

Jane smiled and put her head back on the bench, eyes closed, her mouth half open and her hair falling down over her face.

'I'm sure it will be fine, G. I mean, we wouldn't be here otherwise. I'm more worried about the finances. Now, are you going to come to bed with me?'

'Christ Jane. Don't do this to me now.'

He squeezed her hand for a moment and let it linger before taking it back.

'No, Jane. I like you too much. And it would ruin that now. We made a decision before. Let's just hang on, eh?'

Jane lowered her head and for a moment looked disappointed.

'What happened to us anyway, G?'

'Nothing happened us, Jane. Life happened. That's all. We were young when we met. We're older now.'

'And we're here.'

G stood up, brushing down his jeans.

'Let's get back, will we?'

He looked over her shoulder to where night was coming down over the hills on some place called Quarry Road, then he held out a hand to pull her up from the bench. They walked back slowly and he put his arm around her shoulder and hugged her tight and close so her hair brushed his skin.

Jane leaned her head on G's shoulder.

'You were my best friend for years, G. I miss you.'

G hugged her tighter and stared out across the farm that was sinking in dusk and growing quieter. Protection, wasn't that what it was all about. People just protecting each other against bad thing and evil things that fall upon them for no good reason whatsoever. The way he had protected the girl he first loved as a kid when the bootboy from the neighbouring estate came and took the rope from her and G had hit him so hard with his baseball bat that he heard a crack and was sure he had broken his arm and he knew that one day the bootboys or someone or something was coming to get him. That's the way it goes even if you are working on the side of good. You do good, it comes back. You do something against evil, it will come back twice as hard. In the end you could never really win, but you did have to try.

Sixteen

There was a rope on the breakfast table. A thick rope like the forearm of a sailor. Knotted, coarse and stained. John had put it there the night before when everyone had gone to bed. He knew what he had to do and he knew that the only way to do it was to say nothing that would allow people to try and prepare themselves. There was no other way when it came to killing. Because there is no way of preparing the mind, it can only be done through instinct and self-preservation. Only then can a person's conscience feel settled and John felt they had all spent enough time at the farm for the notion of self-preservation to be instilled in them to some extent.

John's uncle had done the same thing to him one summer on the farm. John came down to breakfast just after six o'clock as usual one morning and had his mind set on going out to the barn to milk the cows. But there on his chair was the rope. He picked it up and looked at it, expecting his uncle to explain the reason for the rope being on his chair. But the Uncle said nothing until he had finished his breakfast, then he turned to John and told him to pick up the rope and follow him outside.

John went out into the paddock and down towards the small shed at the bottom, a shed he had never entered because he had been told never to do so. Now this morning he was being led to the shed by his uncle and on the way the uncle stopped at the barn and turned to John.

'Son, listen to me and listen good. You're going to have to do something and it's not going to be easy. There is no easy way to do it. But you'll understand someday that these things have to be done. Now, let's go and do it together.'

John's uncle led him through the barn gate and towards the pen where they kept Charlie the pig. John loved that pig and both he and the family had cared for him over the last year since they had bought him at the market. They fed him well. They called a vet when he was sick and they'd even allowed John to play with him before he had gotten too big. Charlie became John's friend on the farm. John loved and protected that pig.

But now, as he stood beside him, he knew something terrible was about to happen. He looked up at his uncle and his uncle looked down at him and patted the top of his head. Then suddenly, without warning, he took the rope from John's hands and was in the pen with Charlie. In what seemed like only seconds he had trussed the pig up with the rope, its hind legs tied tight across his chest despite all the kicking and the snorting and squealing that the pig had done.

They used the rope to drag Charlie down the grass and into the shed where a strong beam traversed the ceiling and a second rope dangled from it. This was used to tie Charlie's front legs, and as he was hauled up over the beam his front legs were pulled back and his throat exposed.

From under a long table in the corner of the shed John's uncle pulled out a series of knives wrapped in sackcloth. He pulled out a long knife with a thin blade, oiled and sharpened the night before. Then he placed a bucket beneath Charlie and asked John to hold him tight.

One puncture was all it took to release a spray of blood that eventually became a controllable flow, finishing as tar in the bucket below. For a few moments the pig thrashed and shook and then just twitched as John held it for all he was worth, feeling the last flutters of life leave him and go to wherever pigs go when they die. He stared at the blood in the bucket and watched the pig's eyes grow paler and he wondered where is it that life actually lived, and was it in the blood flowing into the bucket or in the heart of the pig that was slowly beginning to stop pumping. Or was it in the pig's eyes, little windows that were closing shut.

Joey put a hand over her mouth and turned her back.

'I'm not going to watch anymore of this.'

Sara too had a hand over her mouth but she stood her ground.

'Is that it, John? Can we go now?'

John stepped back from the pig and threw the knife on the table, wiping the blood from his face with his sleeve. He looked shaken.

'Do you think it's easy for me? The first pig I killed had a name. I'll never forget him. And no, it's not it. Not at all.'

The work was only just starting now the pig was dead. The first thing was to clean off the hair, and to do that they covered the pig with hay and set it on fire, repeating the burning several times, in between the burnings taking it in turns to scrape the hair from the skin. First John and Ben, then Lofty and G, then Sara and Joey, Pete and Terry, Butcher and Matt and Doc, so on, until the pig was pink and bald. Everyone took it in turns.

Some of the girls had protested, especially Sara and Joey who claimed they were vegetarian and did enough by tending the glasshouses and the vegetable gardens. But John quietly told them the rules again. They had agreed to use whatever was on the farm for their own food. And that meant pigs. And it will mean cows, chickens, pheasant, rabbit, whatever, in fact, wandered onto their farm that could be killed and eaten, as that was the law as it always had been as long as John had known, as his parents had known, and his parents' parents too.

After several fires were made the pig's ears were cooked over the outdoor grill. Butcher cooked them after removing them from the pig. He said it was a ritual and it was a delicacy as you could never actually buy pigs' ears in a shop. John fetched bottles of cold beer and handed them out as Butcher diced the ears up and added salt to go with the cold beer. John and Butcher ate them easily. So did Doc. Terry and Pete tried some, as did Ben, G, Lofty and Matt. But only Jane from the girls ate the ears. She said they were like crisps but was surprised they didn't have the bacon flavour. Butcher laughed at this saying the bacon flavour came later when it was all cured.

The pig weighed over 500 lbs and it took five people to lift it onto the butchering table in the shed. At this stage, John said that it wasn't necessary for everyone to stay and that they had done enough for their first killing. It was after supper and people were tired and there were other things to do. So he asked for volunteers. And Ben, Butcher, Terry and Pete joined John in the shed on that warm afternoon in early July.

But G took John aside and asked to be excused. John raised his eyebrows in surprise. G said that he wouldn't be able to take the butchering. Not today. But he would do it next time. John agreed. Truth was, G hadn't taken the killing of the pig well at all. He had known it was coming and he had tried to prepare his mind for it, but there was no way of doing so, even if he knew that their lives on the farm depended on it. He found it hard to kill animals simply because animals did not commit acts of cruelty on one another. Except the crows. It was okay to kill crows. So John let G go this time.

First to come off were the legs, torn like branches, cut and peeled. The next priority was to get the head off because it required some amount of boiling before making it into sausage. It was hard to crack open the skull. But Butcher did it eventually with a hatchet. With the head gone, they moved on to ripping off the fat. The intestines were piled into a large plastic bucket and the spine was removed and the meat sliced off the bone to be salted. The shanks were frozen for roasting. The tough parts and organs were kept to be put into the pot to boil for several hours for broth. The intestines were kept for making sausage and the guts fed to the dogs. The hooves were dumped and the pen washed out and disinfected. Finally the pig shit was put onto a compost heap so it could go back out onto the earth and put to some good use.

By nine o'clock that evening, just as the sun was tipping itself lower, nothing remained of the pig, and its partner sniffed around in the clean pen, wondering where it had gone to and why.

Seventeen

The pig's death led to some disquiet among the group as few believed the method John had used to kill it was at all humane. Was there no way of stunning the pig first, they asked?

Many suspected that John took some joy in the killing and that he had used old methods because they were more barbaric. His explanation was that he employed methods used by his uncle and they were tried and trusted and had been done for years and that there were reasons why the pig wasn't stunned and that it actually suffered less being killed in this way. His only reservation was the time of year he had done it, and that really he should have waited until it grew colder, but what choice had he got with such a large number of mouths to feed.

But G was concerned the pig's death might be the very thing to upset the balance in the group and that John needed to do something to address it. John assured him that balance in nature was always restored, and neither he nor anyone else on the farm would be able to intervene. But he did promise he was looking at introducing some other animals, one in particular that might help appease those upset by the death of the pig and that one animal, if he did manage to get it at the right price, would not be earmarked for slaughter. But he revealed no more about what this animal might be.

But it was boredom and routine which was also beginning to manifest itself, as the novelty of being liberated for the summer began to wear off. Ben was getting fed up with the milk rounds in the morning and was also getting fed up with heating milk for those who wouldn't drink it straight. It was also him that they complained to about getting sick and having diarrhoea and eventually Doc had to step in and insist on there being an option for fresh milk from the store every morning. So G agreed to swap with Ben as long as Ben agreed to go to the store every morning. G had never gone near a cow in his life and it took him a while to learn how to pull the teats and collect the milk. But afterwards he took to it easy enough, saying later how gentle an animal a cow was and that anyone could do it once they put their mind to it. He even gave the cow a name, though John had made it clear that none of the animals who might potentially be facing slaughter were to be given names. So G kept the name Del to himself, except when he was there on his own in the morning, when he would call the cow by its name;

he was convinced the cow gave up more milk as a consequence. But then John went and got three more cattle and the days of being out on his own were gone. That meant and Butcher, John and Doc were out every morning together.

Terry went and had a fight with Pete, even though they had become the closest of friends on the farm. It was just a simple thing. They had been building up the wall of one of the outhouses and Terry was about to put up another layer of blocks but Pete said it wasn't level, and as he had the spirit level in his hand he was sure to be right. Terry, who was down below the scaffolding, said it would do, and climbed up to put the mortar on. Pete took the trowel out of Terry's hand and threw it on the ground, handing Terry the level to check for himself. Ben, who was working nearby, saw Terry smash the level off the wall and pull himself and Pete off the scaffolding and onto the ground where they began kicking and rolling and punching each other like wild animals.

John finally sorted it, stepping in and pulling them apart, one on each arm like he was picking up sticks, but the pair didn't speak for the rest of that day. It was a sign though that people's nerves were beginning to fray and the intervals between them fraying were growing smaller too.

Trouble of a different kind was brewing from other quarters about which little could be done. As much as they were trying to keep things quiet and themselves to themselves they could do little about the few leakages that were bound to get out every now and again and spread around the town below. Not that the people in the town and beyond didn't have enough to be getting on with but one evening a discussion was raised about becoming involved a bit more in the community and that it might prove beneficial once the business was started. But of all people it was John who wanted nothing to do with the town, which the group thought was unusual. Like shitting on your own doorstep, Terry had said.

People had to go to the town that bit more. Ben was down most mornings getting milk and a few other supplies. Doc needed some medicinal items from the pharmacy. There was the odd visit home for some people who had family birthdays or other occasions that required them to go down and catch the bus. And as much as they wanted to stay put as they had all agreed, it just wasn't completely practical. But the real problem was the cool reception they were getting. And they could insulate themselves as much as they liked, sooner or later something like that was going to niggle.

'Well let's not worry until something happens. And nothing will happen. We can talk all night about possibilities. I know the people here, grew up with them. Besides, everyone's got enough problems of their own down there,' John stated reasonably.

Ben shook his head.

'We've been here for almost two months, John. It's only over the last few weeks, but every time I go down the town I get the looks and stuff.'

'So what? Look back. Who gives a shit?'

'Ah, you know what I mean, John. It's just uncomfortable that's all.'

G was standing at the fireplace with his hands in his pockets, looking pensive.

'Okay, I suggest we just be polite on the visits to the town, not that we're down there much anyway. We are going to need their support at some stage. If somebody comes up to see what's going on, I'll handle them.'

Terry laughed.

'Go for it, you're the one who knows why we're here.'

G stared around at the group who were seated, as always at the end of the night, in the main room, sometimes watching a movie or just reading or drinking wine or a few beers and chatting.

'That's not actually funny, Terry.'

'Sorry.'

'Any ideas about what you're going to say if someone comes up here?'

'Say it like it is, Joey. I mean, what else is there?'

'Why do you think they'll have a problem, G?'

'Nobody said there was a problem, Sara. People just get curious that's all.'

Sara was sitting beside Matt and that was how it had been the last few weeks, with the two having become that bit closer.

'I mean, we've every right to be here, don't we?'

Matt tutted and looked at her.

'It's got nothing to do with rights, Sara.'

'I know that, Matt. But the question is what people are afraid of here? If we barely have any contact with them I don't see why we're even discussing any of this. We've been going fine up until now.'

G looked over at John before he spoke.

'Well let's try and look at this another way, and this is just a guess. We've been here more than two months and we've hardly budged. Apart from John, who they know, we've only made the odd trip to the stores. Any neighbour who keeps to themselves is always going to be the subject of curiosity and gossip. We don't take part in anything that goes on around the place and we don't give anything back. There was the festival there last week and there's community stuff and charity and the church and the whole lot. We do nothing, and there's all this land up here that we're sitting on and people are bound to be wondering what we're up to after the place being unoccupied for so long.'

Pete looked up.

'So you think this land is the real issue then?'

G shrugged and looked over at John again but for an answer this time.

'Let's not get into all that. You all know we turned down deals hundreds of times and it's water under the bridge and I'm not getting back into it. Besides, nobody is concerned about land anymore, you all know that. It's worthless.'

A chair creaked in the darkest corner of the room and Doc leaned forward.

'I think you're all overreacting. You're right, G, we have been here more than two months and that's maybe part of the problem. Cabin fever, and paranoia. Until we're self-sufficient and can close that gate down there once and for all, we have to at least keep people on side. It's that simple. If we remain civilised, sooner or later we'll just be accepted. I mean, has anything actually happened?'

G glanced at Doc who in turn glanced at Matt but Sara got there first.

'There was Matt.'

Jane spun and thumped her hard on the arm.

'Ow! Jesus Christ!'

'What about me?'

'That bump on your head after the party a few weeks ago, it wasn't a fall. Doc reckons someone hit you.'

G took a seat finally.

'Thanks Sara.'

'Who hit me?'

He turned to Pete.

'Don't look at me, Matt. I was in bed.'

Doc leaned forward again.

'It was a possibility, Matt. Nothing has happened since then, if you want me to be more clear.'

Joey shook her head.

'Well, I think the way we just buried the whole event was stupid. I mean, it's something we should have taken more seriously at the time. And I wasn't happy about the way that pig got slaughtered either. I wasn't prepared for that.'

'We've been through all that, Joey.'

'I know Doc but then there is the shooting and hunting all the time, is it really, really necessary? With shops giving away stuff just down the road?'

Sara sighed and looked over at her.

'That's exactly what we've been trying to get at, Joey. Avoiding having to go to the stores for what we can do up here.'

Terry laughed.

'You should see the traps, Joey.'

'Traps?'

'They got bird traps at the back of the barn.'

'For God's sake. Traps?'

John raised his eyes to the heavens and shook his head at G who was on his feet anyway.

'Well that's it then. We leave it alone. Keep our heads down and just stick to our plan,' G said.

'Where are you off to?'

'I'm off to bed, Joey, I'm tired.'

'But we're in the middle of all this.'

'Good. I'm off to bed. There's nothing else to talk about tonight.'

'Jesus Christ, we're talking about him and he just goes off to bed.'

Butcher raised his hand.

'Who do you think is going to visit anyway, John?'

'Don't know. The Gardaí. TV company. Some fucker selling broadband. Priest. Take your pick. Maybe nobody.'

G closed the door quietly behind him and took the stairs two at a time, pulling hard on the bannisters as he heard the group launch into another argument, something about money and the lack of it and what were they going to do when it started to run out. When he got upstairs to his room he pulled over a chair and sat at the open window and took in long deep breaths.

It had been a hot day and the remains of the heat from below came in waves and wafted inside to the bedroom. The moon was hanging low and was the colour of bone. G stared hard at it just as a bird of some sort rose up from the trees near the river. Probably an owl, its wings flashing, caught under the light of the moon as it flew in slow strokes across the fields towards the barn where it disappeared somewhere behind it. G had seen a moon like that before and a bird like that too. It was on a camping trip with Macker and Duff and another guy who G didn't like from the estate.

It was his 16th birthday and they had gone away down the country with a tent between them and cans of food taken from their homes, and Macker had also stolen a bottle of whiskey from his dad which they were going to drink on the first night. Macker had been to the camping spot before with his older brother, so they all depended on him. G had never been away from home like that, not without his parents and not without his sister.

The other guy was called Farrell and he was thrilled with the freedom as they left the city behind. They were sitting up on the top deck of a bus and Farrell was telling them all that freedom had to be taken advantage of and you had to do things that you couldn't normally do at home. Otherwise it was a waste. Everyone had different ideas about what to do. Macker wanted to go shoplifting in one of the villages but that wasn't anything different because they did it all the time. Duff wanted to try and get some more drink from somewhere, cans of cider like the bootboys had. G wanted to find some girls but there wasn't much different about that either. So they all drew straws when they got to the place they were going to camp to see what they would do and it was Farrell who won. And Farrell had brought an air rifle with him and his deal was that everyone had to shoot an animal before they went home. That was his choice. And on the first day he shot a badger. No one had ever seen a badger before so they weren't even sure it was a badger at all. They tied it with wire to a tree near where they were camping and Farrell couldn't stop talking about it.

Macker only managed a rat that had been scraping through the plastic bag they had been using as a bin. It was a pretty easy target and shouldn't have counted, Farrell said. And Duff got hold of a cat that probably belonged to someone and he tied it next to the badger and shot it while it was still alive. But Farrell said it wasn't fair as the cat had no chance and that he had shot the badger when it was moving and he was the winner as far as he was concerned unless G came up with something better.

When it came to G's turn he didn't have the guts though. His target was just a bird sitting about twenty yards away on a branch, as still and peaceful as an angel and with a plumage which had every colour of the rainbow and more. It was the last day and G had avoided the test so far, thinking he was going to get away without doing it at all. But Farrell wouldn't let it go. So when they were all packed and ready to leave, Farrell had forced him. He spotted the bird on the branch waiting for them to leave so it could swoop down and forage among the bits of food that had been left around the camp.

G looked at it and held the gun firm against his right shoulder with the index finger of his right hand on the trigger. He held it there, staring at the target for a full minute until he put the gun down slowly and turned to face the guys who were standing in a row about thirty yards behind him. When the bird finally flew away they hurled all sorts of abuse at him, especially Farrell who bent down and picked up a rock and threw it at G.

G cocked the gun and fired a shot that raised the hair on Farrell's head, and for what seemed like an eternity nobody moved.

Finally Farrell came over to tell him to take it easy, that it was only a game. But he looked scared. More scared than the bird before it flew off and more scared than the badger he had shot or the rat that Macker had blown away or the cat that'd scratched at Duff's arm as he tied it next to the dead badger.

The noise downstairs increased. G could hear the sound of Ben's voice, louder than the rest. And Joey and Sara arguing. Then there was the sound of a door slamming and someone came up the stairs and there was more shouting and banging then finally someone laughed and music came on. Then there were whispers, then silence, and then the night folded over on itself and finally turned that long quarrelsome day over on its head.

Eighteen

On the way out of town, the opposite side to which G and the group had come in and the opposite side to where the ghost estate lay half-built and all stark and desolate, the buildings began to peter out into smaller houses and eventually into rows of cottages that were likely the first dwellings ever, and it was there in the very last one where G had earmarked a bed & breakfast the day he had walked around with Lofty.

He had confided only in Ben that morning before he left and told him what Jane had said, and that he should tell John he had gone home for the night while he took the opportunity to gather as much information as he could. There were questions, G had said, that needed answers, and he wasn't going to get them from John, because John had given as much as he was going to give. Someone had to go and do a bit of prying around before winter set in and the money was all spent and they had crossed the threshold and it was too late to pull out and go their separate ways. At least if things went wrong he could have all the facts to hand and he wouldn't be the only one to blame. Ben agreed. He'd cover him.

The owner of the B&B, a Mrs Doherty, was a widow of about five years, just like G's own mother. She had a son who had gone to work in America and a daughter who had taken a year off college and had yet to send word of returning. The last postcard was from Bali and it came in an envelope with a photograph of herself dressed in all kinds of robes and trinkets and her hair long enough to strangle herself with. The woman showed it to him but G had already seen it because it was on the mantelpiece next to a photo of her son and another photo of herself with her late husband in a silver frame, probably about ten years old.

G smiled as he looked at the picture. Bali. A place that was exotic for some but a hop skip and jump for the Australians or for the hundreds of thousands of Irish living in Australia. He studied the picture and saw that the girl in it was very attractive and he saw joy and love and harmony in her eyes. He saw that there was no way this girl was coming back to a country that would turn her heart to stone if she ever set foot in it again.

'Nice girl.'

Mrs Doherty looked again at the picture and then at some vacant spot in her mind's eye. And she took a long time before she spoke.

'I had hoped she would be coming back to finish her studies. She was supposed to start again in October, but I've given up now. It gets lonely here and even if she does come back I don't think she'd want to live here. What is there here after you've seen the whole world?'

G nodded and put the picture back on the mantelpiece.

'And what about you?'

G hesitated for a moment.

'Well, I'm between college and jobs and decided to hit the road and see if I can pick something up, just to get some money together.'

'Have you had much luck?'

'No. It's fairly dead.'

'Well, I'm not sure what you can find around here. You could try up at Casey's farm. Seems to be getting busy up there. I see the young fella around a bit and heard he's been hiring. Can't imagine how, there's no money in farms these days.'

'Not sure if farm work would suit me.'

'If he'd sold up you could be going up to a hotel now instead. Could have been plenty of jobs up there.'

'Really?'

'There were big plans for this place. But like I say, it's probably just as well. There's a housing estate on the other side of town they can't finish, never mind fill with people.'

'Ghost estate. I saw it. Saw plenty of them.'

'We're a country of ghosts now.'

She looked at the photos on the mantelpiece again of her husband and son and daughter, then stole a glance at herself in the mirror as she fished around in the pocket of her cardigan and pulled out a bunch of keys and handed one to G. G felt the warmth of her hand as he took the key. He found the room at the back of the cottage, which looked out onto a long garden with a high hedge and a view of the mountains off in the distance. He lay on the bed and closed his eyes and there was not a sound to be heard only that of Mrs Doherty downstairs making tea, the clank of a cup on a saucer and the pop of a toaster. G fell asleep.

When he woke it was late afternoon, a lot later than he wanted it to be. Rain dashed the window and G donned a cap, zipped his jacket up to his chin and left with a purpose, taking long strides as he walked with his head down back through the town to the main street and the bank, which was packing its bags and moving on out just like every other business seemed to be doing.

It was just after three o'clock and a small queue stuttered towards two tellers while the desk that had the information sign on it was empty. G stood there anyway and waited, eyeing the few people at the back and finally his gaze got the better of a woman at one of the desks and she approached him but there was no smile, not even a hello or anything.

'I was hoping to speak to the manager.'

Her head turned to one of the doors.

'Do you have an appointment?'

'No. But it's important and it concerns money.'

She frowned and her head turned again back towards the door only this time she went and knocked, then opened it and went inside. When she returned she was smiling.

'You can go in.'

'Mr J Turner General Manager' was written on the door and G walked in with his hand out.

'Mr Turner, thanks for seeing me.'

'Sure. Have a seat.'

Mr Turner sat behind his desk and held his hands together on his lap.

'I'll get to the point very quickly. I'm from up at the Casey farm and I have a proposal for you.'

'Young John Casey's farm?'

'That's right. And I hear he's behind on payments for his mortgage account.'

Mr Turner laughed and leaned forward to grab an elastic band from the top of a tower of files which looked like they were either moving out with the bank too or landing in the skip, then he sat back again and wrapped the band around his fingers.

'I'm sorry, did I get your name?'

'G.'

'G?'

'G.'

'Well, I'm sorry, G, I can only discuss finances with the account holder, which is John.'

'I know that, but soon you and the bank here will be gone and then there'll be even less chance of you talking to John. Because as far as I can see, he's not going to come down here until something gets sorted. So talking to me is the best chance you have of getting something back from all that money you gave him.'

Mr Turner laughed again.

'Are we on the same page here?'

'Mr Turner, all I'm asking for is more time, that's all. He's five months behind in his payments, right? We're coming into August now, right? How about we forget about those last five months and we start all over again next August. We'll continue working as hard as we're working now to turn over some earnings, which by next year will become profit, which we can then begin giving to you. If you don't allow him that window, then we all walk off the farm and you get nothing.'

'That's the proposal?'

'That's a fact. Straight up. I don't see any other way we can do it. Unless you want to be stuck with all that land up there, not to mention all the buildings we are currently working on night and day to restore. Look at it another way, you take his place now it's worth nothing. Nobody will touch it. In a year's time, even if we fail to turn over a profit, it's going to be worth something because it will be a fully operational farm with renovated buildings, all spick and span.'

Mr Turner allowed the elastic to fly.

'You know it makes sense.'

'It's not about sense… G. It's about compliance and contracts and a whole pile of other shit —excuse my French.'

'I understand, but you're moving. Your branch is moving. You're just going to be an even smaller cog in a bigger branch full of hundreds of other small cogs all with the same kind of problem. You've no money coming in. I wouldn't be surprised if those files there are bad debts you're just going to write off and throw in the skip. You draw up an extension for John, today. A new loan agreement. Someone will pick it up tomorrow and I'll get John to sign it and have it back by the end of the week. Just give him until next year.'

'I'm promising nothing. Leave it with me.'

G shook hands with Mr Turner and put his cap back on and zipped his jacket up to his chin again as there was still rain spitting on the window outside. But as he reached the door he stopped.

'Mr Turner, who are the brothers MacMillen?'

The manager stopped and stared then just shook his head.

'Sir, you've complicated my day already.'

'So you've heard of them?'

'I've heard of them. And John's problem, as I see it, is that his uncle didn't sell when he had the chance. Instead he opened a whole can of worms. Then it became our problem.'

He shook his head again.

'Jesus, stubborn bastard.'

'Is that how you see it, really?'

'It's how the whole town sees it. There could have been jobs for everyone in this place if that development went ahead.'

'And where are the brothers now?'

'I don't know... gone. Long gone. Dead. I'll see you tomorrow. I'm sure.'

G used the overhangs on the roofs to dodge as much of the rain as possible as he walked quickly back up the main street and found the post office, which was at the back of the hardware store and had only two of three windows open for business.

'Hello, I have something to post to the brothers MacMillen.'

The woman behind the window looked at him.

'Do you have their address?'

'I have their old address, it's on Quarry Road outside the town, but I'm told they've moved and was looking for a forwarding address.'

The woman looked at G then turned to a computer and began keying in the name but very quickly shook her head.

'No. They're gone. I thought one of them was in a nursing home myself. But I've no address.'

'Do you know anyone who can help me?'

She shook her head and G nodded his and left to dodge the rain under the roof overhangs again, this time having to skip over puddles which were beginning to form at his feet. He crossed the road and made a few turns to get to the garda station, which was a two-storey building with a modern extension at the end of a cul de sac.

The foyer was quiet and the window was closed but there was a bell to ring, so G pressed it and waited, but he had to press it one more time before he heard footsteps and the glass slid back.

'Can I help you?'

'I'm staying up at the old Casey farm just outside the town, and I was wondering if you could give me some information?'

The garda was old but not ranked.

'Casey farm? Heard young John is back up there.'

'Well, I'm one of the friends he has with him. We're helping him get back on his feet.'

The garda smiled.

'Some chance he has. What were you looking for?'

'I was trying to find out about the brothers MacMillen.'

'What about them?'

'I was hoping to find them.'

'Do you know about that case?'

'I know something about it but I was hoping to know more. I googled it but there's not much.'

'That's because there isn't much. The brothers are gone and that case was a mess. But it's closed and settled and that's all there is to it. The Caseys got what they wanted anyway, what do you want to go stirring it up now for?'

'I've a feeling they're not gone.'

'Who?'

'The brothers.'

'They're gone. They're gone. One of them is even dead, I heard.'

'Well, can you help me get some more information?'

'No. There's nothing else to be said about that whole affair. And if the Caseys sold up like everyone else, there'd have been no case and probably a thriving town and community too.'

'What if I told you we're being threatened.'

'By who?'

'The brothers.'

The garda put his hand on the glass and slid it back shut.

'If we were being threatened, could you help us?'

G waited for an answer but heard only footsteps disappearing down the hall.

Quarry Road was a steep hill with the asphalt peeling away from the surface leaving loose gravel and potholes. G had his iPhone out and was looking at a map on the screen which was getting pelted with drops of rain, not only from the blanket of dark cloud but by even bigger drops from the trees as he made his way upwards. When he reached a bend in the road he'd stop and look and get his bearings and he soon realised that Quarry Road wound around the back of Casey's farm.

At the top of the hill a narrow lane with a stripe of grass down the middle cut through the hedgerows to the left. This was it. The brothers' old farm. G walked down the lane and came to a house at the end of it, a large paddock, fenced off, and a small barn, nothing like the size of what John had up at his farm.

The walls of the house were the colour of the rain clouds and the windows looked to be boarded up. But when G got closer he realised they weren't boarded up at all, with the sheets of wood just propped against the frames and the nails long pulled out and scattered on the ground and rusted. In the small barn at the back two dogs barked and there were fresh tyre marks in the muck leading from the house through the gate and away over the fields. G tried the front door and it opened out onto a hall with soiled carpet and the door to a room on the left was ajar. He stood in the doorway hearing the rain pounding on the roof above him and figured if nobody lived there anymore the door should have been locked. And if somebody did live there the door should have been locked. *What the hell is the door doing open?*

He stepped in slowly and went into the room on the left where a couch was pulled up in front of the fireplace and in the grate sat a mound of ash. He kicked it with his boot and it crumbled in a topple of greys and browns and dark lumps of spent coal. Not like the hard crusted mound in John's fireplace the first day he had visited which had been sitting there months.

The sound of an engine in the distance froze G where he stood. He pulled his boot out of the ash, stepped backwards to the hall door, slammed it shut and turned and ran, skipping over puddles and skidding and threatening to fall over with the gravel giving way under foot. And behind him the sound of the engine came closer and closer until he got too far away to hear it.

That evening G ate with Mrs Doherty. She had offered when she saw him return soaked through and dripping with rain. He was cold and shaken and hungry and there was a smell of roast chicken in the kitchen where warm steam filled the air. G said he would pay extra for the meal but Mrs Doherty wouldn't hear of it. So after a shower and a change of clothes, he sat at the table and ate roast chicken with roast potatoes, stuffing and cauliflower that was soft and covered with gravy. Mrs Doherty spoke mostly about her son and daughter and each tale brought the beginnings of a tear, so G would smile and comment on how wonderful it was to have such fine memories and this would stop the tears from falling.

With dinner done and his appetite sated G realised he had a thirst and so left the house to go in search of a quiet bar to sit at for the evening. The rain had stopped but the air was wet, fuzzing the street lamps which cast a thick grainy light on the streets. Most of the shopfronts had their display lamps switched off and each bar G passed was closed up and dead. He thought about finding the place John had taken him to but that was a little way out of town and he didn't feel much like walking after the day he'd had.

Then he spotted a sign on a wall at the entrance to a laneway which said 'Sweeney's Pub' and an arrow pointed into the lane, so G followed it and saw a small premises with a single table and a couple of chairs outside all dripping wet with rain. He pushed the door open and peered inside and if the pub wasn't dead that night then it didn't have many nights left before it went west with the rest of them. It was dark in there too, the bar itself seeming to be the only area fully lit with side lights barely illuminating the tables and the corners where a few small groups of men sat.

G went directly to the corner of the bar just inside the door and pulled out a stool and sat on it, propping his legs on the iron piece running underneath. He looked up at the barman, an old guy who was staring at him from the far end of the bar as he pulled a pint for another customer. Finally he came over and raised his head slightly.

'Now, what can I get you?'

'Guinness.'

The barman nodded and smiled and repeated the word 'Guinness' to himself as he walked to the tap and began to pour.

'You can give me a large whiskey too there.'

'Water?'

'Just ice.'

'Just ice.'

The whiskey was placed in front of him, the colour of honey. The ice began to split in the glass and G gave it shake and downed half of it as the pint arrived. He drank it quickly, in just three turns and held the empty glass up at the barman for another.

There was a man seated at the end of the bar on his own drinking lager and he looked at G.

'Have you got a hole in that glass?'

The man laughed after he'd said it and the barman laughed with him, so too did G.

'No, just thirsty. Nice pint.'

'Never been here before so?'

'No, first time. Just passing through, saw the pub and—'

'You were a bit thirsty.'

G shrugged.

'That's it.'

G paid the barman and picked up the fresh pint and stared at it before taking a small sip.

'Is there a hole in that one?'

G laughed and downed a good third.

'Where did you get such a thirst anyway?'

'Will you leave my customers alone? God knows I fecking need them.'

The barman shook his head as he lifted the hatch at the back of the bar and stooped and groaned to get under it. Then he went out into the bar to go and collect glasses.

'Maybe you've been working hard. Is that why you're thirsty?'

The man suddenly leaned forward and began whispering.

'Do you take me for an eejit?'

G raised his hands in a small shrug. It was then his eyes were diverted to someone in a corner of the bar sitting with his back to him. Big guy with a big shadow.

'We could all have been working up there. You shower of bastards.'

The man nodded the top of his glass at G a few times then raised it to his lips finally taking his eyes off him as the barman returned. G picked up his glass and began drinking, not too fast, just moderately. Although the bar had gone quiet again he could hear the slow steady thump of a boot like a funeral march tapping out from the corner of the bar where the big guy sat.

He ordered another whiskey and knocked it back, the ice hitting his teeth as the man at the end of the bar slammed his empty on the wood and raised his hand.

'Give us another lager. Are you having another pint MacMillen?'

The big guy turned.

'Aye. Get us another.'

G's heart raced and he tumbled off the bar stool and out into the laneway and stopped to lean against the cold metal of a lamppost. Then he ran quickly back to the house, lit by a single bulb over the doorway, and opened the hall door quietly. He crept up the stairs to the room at the back which looked out over the dark fields and beyond at the purple mountains.

Nineteen

The next morning G awoke early in a strange bed in a strange house with darkness still lingering. He wanted to be back at the farm before breakfast and get up to speed with everyone's plans for the day ahead. He pulled out some money from his wallet to leave on the table downstairs before he left, but then he heard Mrs Doherty going down ahead of him and there came the sound of the tap and the kettle and the clink of cups and saucers.

'Look, son. I know you're from up at the farm.'

She handed G a cup of tea and put a plate on the table with brown bread, butter and jam.

'Are you sure you won't have anything else to eat?'

'No, no. This is fine.'

'If you want my advice, you'd be better off away from here. You're young, you've no ties, away you go and find a better life somewhere else.'

'We found a better life. And it was ours. But it's looking like we can't have it.'

'Nothing is ever going to be all yours, son. There are always those who will take and you'll always end up giving.'

G finished his tea and stood to go.

'Do you know anything more about the brothers MacMillen?'

'I knew of them. They're gone now. Long gone.'

'That's what I keep hearing. Do you know who can help us up there if we get into trouble?'

'Just don't let it come to that.'

When G was out on the road he heard the door close shut and found himself all alone with the chill and the heavy fog that clung to countryside in large blankets. He walked ahead squinting down the main street guided by the light from lampposts, one by one, until at the end of the town they ran out into the quiet country road to be replaced by the trees.

G cursed and swore as the fog grew thicker on the road up to the farm, the click of his boots and the trickle of water in the ditches on both sides amplified in the still air. Over the brow of the hill the sun was splitting the horizon and he aimed for that as he walked. Click. Click. Scrape. Click. The sound of his boot heels on the wet grit.

Suddenly he stopped and turned to look back the way he came but with the fog and the grey light he couldn't see more than a hundred yards, if that. But that didn't stop him from hearing and he swore there was another set of footsteps coming up the hill behind him, slower in pace and wider apart. He stalled and they stalled too; he moved and they moved with him.

He picked up his pace as he ploughed upwards, the town shrinking behind him as he marched the four long lonely miles up towards the farm with the boots marching behind him until he reached the humpbacked bridge just before the gate. Then the footsteps behind him stopped. Just like that. G turned, but he could still see nothing through the fog even though dawn was breaking it up.

He leaned against the bridge, getting his breath back, and dropped a spit over the side into the gurgling waters below. Despite the chill he was sweating and his clothes stuck to his skin, so he loosened his jacket as he reached the farm but was stopped from going any further by a large wooden gate that had not been there the previous morning when he left. Gone were the old iron gates with bars buckled and eaten by rust, there now hung one solid wooden gate with firm hinges keeping it posted to the concrete pillar on one side and with a handle and a great big bolt keeping it safe on the other.

It wasn't just the gate that had stopped G in his tracks but what sat on top of it, slightly off centre to the left. A large figure of an angel, bold and beautiful, almost impeding the direct view down the laneway where the tops of trees met from both sides to form a tunnel. G had seen many images of this figure and heard many a word uttered in his name. But now he sat moulded from a dark mahogany, bent forward with his head tilted to one side and a bow and arrow on his back. G felt the carvings with his hand, felt the grain of the wood, worn and smooth with the point on the arrow filed to an edge. He pushed the gate open and strolled down the lane with the trees dripping and with some relief now the town was behind him, and the fog too.

It was approaching seven o'clock and John was already there in the garden with a large wheelbarrow full of so much material G couldn't even guess what it was. He waved and grinned as G approached the house, coming up to greet him with a warm extended hand.

'So what do you think?'

'The angel on the gate?'

'Not any angel, my lad. That's Gabriel, the archangel.'

'It's a nice touch, John. So, where did you find him?'

'Terry and Peter dug him out of the attic a few weeks ago actually. Been working on it up there. The uncle carved him out of a piece of mahogany years ago and he had always been part of the farm until the uncle died, then it got buried in the attic. No one else liked it but myself. Beautiful piece of work. Terry wasn't mad on the idea but he cleaned it up, gave it a sand and varnish and there it is.'

'Was anyone mad on the idea? It's in the rules, John. No religious paraphernalia.'

John looked down the lane and shrugged slightly.

'Thing is, Gabriel is mentioned by Christians and Muslims, did you know that? Said to have appeared to both Mohammed and Mary. Funny, isn't it?'

'Couldn't give a shit either way, to be honest. Where did the gate come from?'

G turned back to look down the lane at the gate and the angel on top with its back turned on the farm.

'He's got a bow and arrow on his back. Don't know why that was put there. I suppose he was a warrior. Ever since I was a kid I loved that angel. He sat on a small pedestal over in the far side of the garden there, just under the trees. You'd hardly have seen him. But I used to go over and sit beside him when I felt a bit lost or afraid. It was my little spot of safety and comfort. But I was just a kid.'

'Sure, John. Let's leave him alone so.'

G put a hand on John's shoulder and led him towards the steps up to the front door of the farm.

'How was your day yesterday? Ben said you were to head home. Wasn't expecting you back so soon.'

'Wasn't at home, John.'

'Where did you go?'

'Down the town. Stayed in a local B&B.'

'What did you that for? Sure were we not talking about all that the other night?'

'Turns out you're not the most popular guy around here. Neither was your uncle for sitting on the land.'

'I could have told you that.'

'But you didn't, and that's why I went down. But that's not the real worry.'

John stopped walking.

'What is?'

'Think those brothers are back.'

'The brothers MacMillen?'

'That's right. Think they're back in these parts.'

'They're gone, G. Dead I thought.'

'So I keep hearing. Well unless there's MacMillens' ghosts living in the house and drinking pints in Sweeney's pub.'

'Sweeney's pub?'

'Well, I could have been mistaken on that one. I was drinking whiskies quick. But there were a couple of guys in there, one big guy with a big shadow. Stamping his boot. Bang. And I'm sure someone called him MacMillen. Either way, there's someone living in their old house up on Quarry Road. No doubt about that.'

'Ah Jesus, what else did you get up to?'

'Went into the bank, John.'

'For what?'

'To buy you more time. You were never going to do it. Were you?'

G had his hand on John's shoulder and squeezed it gently at first, then a little harder.

'I was trying to get on top of it.'

'But you didn't. I've got to go back down later on and see if I can pick up a new agreement. Might have got an extension. And you can pray to your angel there that we did. Otherwise we're all off. You got to be more upfront, John. I put Jane in there because I knew she wouldn't mess about. The finances are in shit.'

'I know. But we're getting there.'

G let go his shoulder and carried on walking.

'Anyway, like I said, we could have other things to worry about. I think someone followed me up here this morning too.'

'Who?'

'Christ, I don't know. I couldn't see him well enough. I could hear him though. I could hear his boots, like the ones last night in the bar stamping on the floor. And I could sense him. You taught me all about that, and I learned well. And I'm not lying.'

They went in through the front door to the hall and stopped, aware that their voices could be carried downstairs to the breakfast table.

'G, there's something you have to trust me on for the moment. And I'm going to ask you for that much.'

'How many more secrets are there to this place?'

'It's got its history, but like we said, we're looking forward now. Just trust me. You're on good ground.'

G closed the door behind him and stepped in, feeling the ground beneath him change from wood to something soft. He looked down and noticed he was standing on a huge rug instead of the bare boards he had got so used to walking on, with the sound of the creaking audible from the top to the bottom of the house. Now this rug covered almost the entire floor and was sure to dampen the thump of the sturdiest boot. G stamped down hard on it to see.

'Christ, what are you trying to do? Put the thing through the boards?'

'Where did you get it?'

'It was in the attic as well. Lot of stuff up there we can put to use. Come on in here.'

John led him into the second biggest room which thus far had no real use apart from people taking advantage of the privacy and space it allowed.

'We've a new plan for these rooms. Lounge room. We can have our meetings in the evenings in here. Make it more comfortable.'

He then moved across to the room opposite that looked out onto the front garden, pushing the door open.

'This is to be the recreation room.'

G looked in and noticed first the makings of a large structure over in the corner.

'What's that there?'

'That's going to be our bar. There's a sale in one of the pubs on Saturday morning. Closed for good. Reckon we can pick up a few stools, couple of tables, glasses and taps and so on. Do a proper job. They've got an old pool table down there too.'

'We don't need a pool table, do we?'

'They want it. It's their money and time too.'

'So what else have you got in mind for the place then?'

'Down the way, next to the office, we'll be putting the library and conference room in there.'

'Conference room?'

'For want of a better word. Get some desks and chairs, move the PCs in, get a whiteboard, floor to ceiling shelves for books, all that. That's what you wanted, isn't it?'

'It's perfect, John. Perfect.'

John nodded and whispered.

'Trust me, G.'

Later that afternoon Joey ran from the edge of the paddock where the soft fruit had been planted and burst in through the back door to the kitchen where Sara and Jane were making supper. She had a box under her arm and threw it down on the counter next to Sara who had her sleeves rolled up and was washing vegetables in the large ceramic sink.

'Give them a wash too.'

There was something special about their first crop of strawberries though it seemed like such a simple everyday thing in the real world. But when they all sat round the table after supper and ate them straight from a large bowl, with their fingers and faces covered in the red juice, it felt like the bond between them had grown that bit stronger with the fruit of their labours literally there in front of them. And it wiped away the death of the pig and the hunting and shooting and G's traps, and even the group's isolation from the rest of the town was forgotten now that their own harvest was coming in from the fields. And over the next few weeks there was a lot more where that fruit came from. Heads of lettuce, onions, tomatoes, cabbage from the paddock, herbs from the herb garden outside the kitchen, carrots, celery and potatoes. It got to the point where they began to feel spoiled, guilty almost at having so much food available on their own doorstep for nothing, no money had to change hands to put food on their table.

John had also been working hard at bringing other parts of the farm up to a more cultivated level, with a perchery he had been building out at the barn almost finished. All it needed was a trip to the market with

Butcher to buy the hens. The perchery would allow the birds to be kept indoors and warm in a large shed on several shelves and with floor space littered with wood shavings below. An outside area had been fenced off into the barnyard which meant they had room to roam too. These hens would provide eggs and if the feeding was up to standard they could be feasibly labelled as organic and not just free range.

John was also going to get hold of chickens for meat, chickens which would only have a lifespan on the farm of about eight weeks before they would be killed. Nobody believed that any animal would only be allowed to live on the farm for such a short space of time, but John simply found that amusing. The chicken isn't aware of how short life is for them. Neither was the pig, who could expect to have a good life on the farm for at least a year. The cows will last for several years and the sheep that John had got some time ago that were grazing quietly in one of the far fields would live for possibly seven years. A fly lives for only 24 hours and doesn't know any better. It was all relative.

One evening however, John came to G with his rifle over his shoulder to ask him to help on a search. One of his sheep was missing and he feared it might have been attacked by dogs or it could have wandered off somewhere and gotten lost in the hills. G gladly obliged and was happy to have something different to do, even if the task was less than savoury.

John was quiet as he led the way down with his two dogs towards the fallow field and beyond to a smaller field that worked its way up the hillside, a rocky field given over to the few sheep to graze, heavily overgrown with a large variety of wild flower. The sheep were doing a good job at getting through most of the long grass but John had wanted to get a goat also to rid the area of the thistles and other heavy foliage. He had put it to the group during one of the evening meetings, but Joey had protested. She was terrified of goats. She said they reminded her somehow of the devil and maybe it was just the horns, or possibly the eyes, which were the most human of any animal. Maybe it was that.

The whole group laughed at the notion until Sara piped up and said that there was nothing wrong with having fears of different animals and wasn't she herself afraid of reptiles and it wasn't just that some were loaded with poison but it was because of their long tongues. And G had a fear of crows. And spiders, G added, in an effort to support Joey, who seemed genuinely upset at the idea of a goat wandering loose on the farm. So John would have to do without the goat and cut the thistles himself with a scythe.

It was getting quite late when they headed over the hillside field and a thin veil of drizzle began to spray their faces. John stood on top of a rock and counted the sheep once more and confirmed that one was indeed still missing. He looked around and cursed to himself, wondering which direction to begin the search and without a word just took off down the hill with both dogs, climbing over the fence and towards the wooded area near the river. He said nothing to G, walking quickly ahead using the rifle to poke at heavier growth and thistle along the way.

Suddenly the dogs began barking and John heard a sound coming from a group of whin bushes close to a rocky outcrop. He stopped and held a hand up to hold G who was making a meal of getting through the thicker growth. Then he heard it again and this time ran in the right direction and quickly discovered on the ground beneath the bushes the lost sheep with one leg badly broken just below the knee. The animal looked to be on the verge of exhaustion and John bent down slowly and began patting it just at the back of the neck and below the ears, whispering to it quietly in an effort to calm it down as it had been kicking and kicking to try and pull itself up, the torn grass and muck at its hooves evidence of that.

John stood back up and shook his head.

'There's nothing we can do for the poor girl now, G.'

G looked down at the sheep and went to pet it himself but John stopped him.

'Don't do that.'

'Why not?'

'The poor thing is crawling. Roll her over there a bit if you want to see but I wouldn't do that either.'

'Crawling with what?'

'Maggots, G.'

'Maggots? I thought they went after dead animals.'

'They'll go after animals when they know they're about to die as well, G. She's obviously being lying on her side for a day or two now and with the damp ground she's started to rot. Poor thing. Poor thing didn't deserve to die like this. I should have been more careful.'

'It wasn't your fault, John.'

'I still should have been more careful. I hadn't been looking after them as much as I should have. You tend to think sheep will manage just fine. They're good animals. But then this happens.'

John suddenly cocked his rifle.

'Do you have to?'

'No other way. You go on. I'll come back later with Butcher and we'll rope her up and get rid of her properly.'

G walked back down the hill through the other sheep that parted slowly like clouds, then he heard the shot ring out and the other sheep jumped just as he did. He paused and waited for John as the rain began to grow heavier and the sheep moved around him looking for shelter on the windswept hill.

John came over the fence looking downcast and G swore he was wiping his eyes, but maybe it was just the rain. He patted G on the back and thanked him and moved on towards the farmhouse with the lights visible in the distance. G allowed John the time to say nothing for a good stretch until they got closer to the barn.

'Sorry about the sheep, John.'

'Nature is cruel, you see, G. It doesn't respect you once you're on the way out. It'll carry on doing its thing. No matter whether you're human, animal or maggot. Nature treats you the same way.'

'So what do you have to do with the carcass?'

'Well, large numbers would have to be collected and incinerated but we can either do that ourselves with the one sheep or we can bury her. You have to be careful doing that though, 'cos you can't have her rotting into the water table. I'll burn her, it's the easiest and cleanest way of doing it.'

When they got back to the yard it was getting darker and John took a large torch and some rope from the barnyard and went to fetch Butcher. Together, they made the journey back over the hill to get the body of the dead sheep, where they carefully tied her up and took her back to the yard where John made a large pyre soaked in diesel to destroy the carcass.

Butcher stood back as the flames lit the sky.

'Can't stand the smell of burning animals, John. Could you not have buried it?'

'I hate to think of the poor thing being eaten by maggots.'

Butcher laughed.

'But sure we're all going to be eaten by maggots, John.'

John took a spade and shoved the carcass further onto the embers.

'Maybe we deserve it, Butcher. That poor thing doesn't. Come on, get another spade there and help us.'

Butcher laughed again and shook his head then he took another spade from the barn and helped mix the red hot embers with the blackened carcass of the sheep until eventually all that was left was a mound of black ash.

Twenty

It was a hot day in early September when their first official visitor arrived. Nobody heard him coming because he had walked the four miles up rather than drive and it wasn't until Sara came out from the kitchen to call G who had been mixing plaster with Terry, Pete and Lofty at the outhouses that they knew someone was there. G looked up and saw Jane standing at the small gate in the hedge with a look of some urgency on her face as she pointed behind her, over her shoulder, then quickly went back inside.

Terry was on top of the scaffolding and had a good view out into the lawn at the front.

'I think we've a visitor.'

'I know. I'll go.'

G put down his trowel and washed his hands at the tap on the wall then walked up to the house sluggishly in the midday heat. He passed through the gap in the hedges and round the corner to where a man was standing at the steps of the front door of the house, admiring the lawn which John had planted out in beds of flower and shrubbery all abloom now in a rainbow of colour.

G squinted against the light of the sun, even harsher at the front of the farm than at the back. Then he hesitated. A man dressed in black stood against the sun and he turned and looked at G. He nodded at the flowerbeds.

'Nice.'

'Yeah, but they've not got long left. Be autumn soon.'

'Still. Lovely to see a garden like that. I'm Father Donelan.'

The priest put out his hand and G took it and was met by a firm grip that lasted longer than necessary.

'G.'

'Yes. The girl in the kitchen told me.'

Just at that moment Sara appeared up the steps of the kitchen with a jug of their homemade lemonade and two glasses on a tray which she put over on the bench beneath the trees.

'Your own?'

'The lemonade is but the lemons aren't. Maybe next year.'

They both sat down and G poured lemonade into the two glasses, allowing chunks of ice to tumble too.

'What can I do for you?'

'Well I have my habit of visiting newcomers to try and welcome them to the community. I was looking for John anyway. Is he here?'

'No, he's out doing the rounds somewhere.'

'Right. I used to come up here quite a lot, you know, before his uncle died. John was baptised here, in our church. But it's been a while since I've seen him now.'

'Well, he's back in business.'

'So I believe. Tough times though, to be getting a business like this together.'

'Well, he's got a lot of help.'

'So I see. That's really why I'm here actually. We've been getting this community project off the ground down in the town, you might have heard about these types of things springing up, with the recession and so many people finding it difficult to cope. There's no collecting money, it's just people using their knowledge and skills to help others out. Home help, fixing stuff, plumbing and electrics, roofing, the little jobs people can't afford to get done anymore. We have a database of givers and receivers and we match them up. We're a bit short of givers though.'

'That's always the way.'

'Well, with a bunch of youngsters up here, skilled and knowledgeable and with time on your hands, I thought you could help us out.'

'Well, time is something we don't have, I'm afraid. We don't have a whole lot else either, but we definitely don't have a lot of time. You go and ask Mr Turner down there in the bank and he'll confirm that for you. He's counting every day we have as well as every penny.'

The priest put his glass back down on the tray as the ice melted to water and the water began to evaporate in the heat.

'I see. So what do you hope to achieve here?'

'Live. Make a living.'

'So this is your little Garden of Eden then?'

'No, it's a farm. And we aim to get it back up and running again. We really would love to help out down in the town but the best way we can do that is to get this business going and who knows, there might even be jobs up here come next summer.'

'I think that chance has come and gone.'

'You're referring to the Caseys' refusal to part with their land.'

'It was a golden opportunity.'

G stood and began walking slowly back down the laneway as the figure of Gabriel came into view with his back turned. The priest nodded at it as he approached.

'And who might this be anyway?'

'Supposed to be Gabriel.'

'And he's going to watch over you, is he?'

'It belonged to John's uncle. I think it used to sit in the garden.'

'Well, if you want to reconsider what I asked you, I'd be grateful.'

'I'll put it to the group this week.'

The priest turned to walk back down the hill putting

a hand up in front of his eyes to shield them from the sun but G stopped him.

'Did you know the brothers MacMillen?'

He turned keeping his hand over his eyes.

'The brothers? Sure they're long gone. Dead, I believe.'

'So I keep hearing. Did you bury them?'

'Can't say I did. Why?'

'Well, I think they've come back. I'm wondering what they might be back for, but nobody will tell me.'

'You know what the worst part about taking charge of things is? You find you're on your own. But you can change all that.'

'Thanks, Father'

G watched him as he walked down the road, disappearing over the bridge into a haze then he closed the gate firmly and kicked the bolt across the bottom with his boot, securing it fast.

'That'll keep the lot of them out. Bastards!'

Ben had taken over his spot on the outhouses while he was with the priest and he dropped what he was doing and met him coming through the gate.

'Well?'

'The parish priest.'

'What did he want exactly?'

'Visiting John. And he wants us to go down there and help out on this community project. Don't have time for that, and besides, why should we? From what I gather, they don't like us and they certainly never liked the Caseys.'

'Fuck them so.'

'The man was all right, Ben. He had to come up at some stage, he's been coming here for years. And if he needs help, he needs help. Only we never asked for it, did we? Managed okay.'

'Hope we never will. But it's a different thing here, G, isn't it? We don't know about the land, about territory.'

G spat on the ground and looked over towards the glasshouses.

'Ah, I've heard all about the bloody land from John. I'm sick of it. Tell us Ben, what's Matt doing over in the glasshouses? Thought he was supposed to be over here this week.'

'Think he switched.'

'Switched?'

'When you were away the other day, he sort of put himself on it.'

G glanced back over at Matt who was standing in the doorway of the glasshouse having a smoke and chatting to Sara who was up to her elbows in a bucket of tomatoes.

'Right, well let's get these walls finished before supper then.'

Twenty-one

With the sky bruising in the west there was just enough light remaining to see inside the glasshouse, but if G's suspicions were right he would find what he was looking for easily enough just by feeling around in the clay with his hands.

With the girls gone back inside, he went over across the paddock to the first glasshouse where Matt had been earlier and opened the door. He was hit straight away by a wall of heat and the acrid smell from the rows of tomato plants hung with chord from the struts above. He closed the door and followed the line of heads which bobbed all the way down to the back, because if he was Matt, that's exactly where he would have gone.

In the half-light the place looked macabre, with twisted limbs and grotesque shapes and the buzz of insects up under ceiling of glass. G picked up a bucket used for collecting the tomatoes and moved quickly down into the heart of the greenhouse pushing the branches aside as he walked and feeling them brush back against him in return.

About two-thirds of the way down he fell to his knees and slowly put the palm of his hand into the moist soil and scooped up what was taking root between the tomato plants. Then he stood up slowly and walked back towards the grey light at the open doorway.

They were all seated around the large table in the kitchen eating supper, and there were two bottles of red wine open at either end. When G came he pushed one aside and looked directly at Matt. He had something in his hand but he waited for Matt to look up, which he did, sidling down along the bench in at the alcove.

'Have a seat there, G. Good grub.'

G threw the contents of his hand down on the table where the wine bottle had been and all eyes looked up as about a dozen or so small green plants landed and scattered on the wood. Matt jumped forward and swept them together in front of him.

'It's not what you think.'

'Haven't got to the thinking yet, Matt. Had just been doing the looking. Thought maybe you could save me too by coming out and saying it. I just spent the morning with the priest telling him we had no time to help in his community then I go and find this shit. It could have been the cops for Christ sake.'

John leaned over and picked up one of the small plants

'Didn't know you could grow that here.'

'After the summer we've had, he could grow a fucking poppy field.'

Matt said nothing but let his head fall as took his knife to his plate and began scraping it idly.

'Anyone else involved in this? Sara? Joey?'

'It was nothing to do with them. Or anyone else. A mate of mine gave me the stuff to grow. I didn't think it'd work actually.'

'But surely the girls knew about it. They work in the bloody place every day.'

'It was nothing to do with them, I said. It was about making some money. You'd clear in a week what those tomatoes and onions and shit would take months to earn. Anyway, I wanted to have some stuff here seeing as we don't get out much.'

G wiped his hands on his overalls and picked up the wine bottle and took a long swig from the neck, then wiped his mouth with his sleeve.

'Right, Matt, well that's it. Pack up. You're gone tomorrow.'

When G had slammed the door, Matt had yet to look up and there was a long pause before anyone spoke, but Lofty who was sitting opposite was first.

'That was a bit stupid now, Matt. It was also pretty bloody selfish.'

Matt raised his eyebrows quickly but didn't answer. But Sara beside him put a hand on his knee.

'I don't think he should be kicked out though, Lofty.'

'Sara, I don't think you're in a position to argue. Yourself and Joey must have known about that shit.'

Matt finally threw the knife down.

'They did. But I asked them to look the other way. It's my fault. I take responsibility. I thought this place was supposed to liberate us from all this crap. Has anyone else got anything to say? Am I on my own here? Ben?'

'We're still inside the law, Matt. That was one of the first things we said, way back in the hall in the college. The rules are there. We all made them. We don't do anything here that could jeopardise the existence of the project. That's it. Whatever about your own stuff. This is supply. We all go down.'

Terry reached for the wine bottle and poured liberally into a mug he had just been drinking tea from.

'How much of it have you got tucked away down there, Matt?'

'Not that much really. I'd only a few packs of seeds. It was supposed to take up to twelve weeks to grow but the bloody stuff has rocketed. Kind of surprised me.'

'Well, the first thing you do tomorrow is go down there with a shovel and dig it up. Then we can burn the lot of it. We can have one big blow out among ourselves at the same time. Might be worth it. Eh, Doc? You can come down too and get a bit of a buzz.'

Doc smirked.

'The way I see it, Matt, is that we always knew this was going to be a risk. The chances of it working are slim. But, there was a still a chance we would be proven wrong. Now something like this causes problems, because G has told you to leave. Which means that some might agree and others not. Now what we don't need is for this thing to turn into chaos and for us all to be fighting amongst ourselves. Because I can see that people here are starting to take sides already. And I can tell you, I'm with G on this one.'

Sara took her hand from Matt's knee and slammed it on the table.

'But it's only a bit of dope for Christ's sake. I mean, I for one didn't come down here to have G telling us what to do!'

Butcher raised his hand and sighs filled the room.

'Well, I say we have a vote. I mean, that's what we do.'

Sara looked at him.

'Now?'

'Why not?'

Matt shook his head and pulled out a pack of tobacco and papers and rolled a cigarette on his plate.

'Christ. I mean what happened to this great escape deal we were all promised? Now I'm the subject of a vote for God's sake.'

John leaned over and took Matt's plate and brushed the tobacco flakes over on to his lap.

'Well, have it your way then. Pack up and fuck off. Because if you're going to put the rest of us in jeopardy and bring my farm down I'll take you out myself.'

'Jesus, take it easy. All right then, I'm sorry. Look, I love it here and I fucked up. But there are plenty of laws being broken all the time.'

'Like what?'

'Well, fires for one thing. It's illegal to be incinerating the amount of shit that you do now, John.'

'Not true.'

'And killing animals like that. That's not right.'

'It's not illegal.'

Matt stubbed his cigarette, held his hands up and stood and whipped a bottle of wine from the counter as he left. They could hear the creak of the stairs as he climbed and the sound of a door closing at the top. Doc stood and raised his hand.

'It's an aye for me, whoever is counting.'

Then he left as Sara raised her hand.

'I'll count. And it's a no for me. Joey?'

'No.'

'Pete?'

'Aye.'

'Terry?'

'Sorry. I liked Matt, but it's an aye for me.'

'Jane?'

'Aye.'

'Butcher?'

'I like Matt too. But he did fuck all. So it's an aye.'

'Ben?'

'Aye.'

'Lofty?'

'I don't know. I liked him too.'

'Just give us an answer, Lofty.'

'Aye.'

'John?'

'Fuck him.'

'So that's an aye, then. What about G?'

Ben laughed.

'I think we know what G thinks. Now who is going to tell Matt?'

G was out on the lawn watching night move across the sky like spilt ink. He'd been in the barn and had taken a bottle of cider from one of the crates. He was drinking it by the neck quick, burping fizzy apple, keen to get it down and get back inside. He was about to turn when something caught his eye down at the trees near the river, something painted into the shadows that didn't belong. He stared and whatever it was seemed to stare back then it moved again slowly further into the trees and just about out of sight.

G felt that cold hand on his shoulder pulling him back to the light at the back door but he stood his ground to see if he could make any sense of what it was. Then he heard a sound, wood knocking on wood or maybe it was metal on wood but whatever it was it kept a slow and steady rhythm and it was loud and it wasn't letting up. So G turned then, and not only did he turn but he ran as he did so, lobbing the bottle into the grass and making his way in through the back door to the kitchen where the group had dispersed for the night and there was nothing but the hum of the fluorescent strip left on over the counter and the sudden chime of the clock in the hall.

Twenty-two

G's mother had described it as a darkness that had come over her. You spend almost all of your life with someone and then they are gone. She could hear a door closing at the back of her head, then all that was left were memories that seemed to be cruel and unfair rather than precious like the moments that inspired them.

G found him where he'd fallen just a couple of hundred yards from the churchyard on his way back from morning mass. He was slumped against a wall at the entrance to a narrow lane where the back gates to people's houses had been boarded and bricked up. The lane had become a hangout for drunks and junkies and people that morning had walked past G's father figuring he was just one of them. But he wasn't. He was somebody's father and he had been a good father too, even if he had slipped off the rails the last few years. And he was somebody's wife and she had loved him the whole way but he was gone and it was as if a darkness had come over the house. And for many nights after that G would lie awake in nothing but darkness afraid and alone until one night he slept clean through without any disturbed dreams and woke to the morning sun cracking the curtains at the sides. Then he realised that morning follows night and it had always been like that and it always would be.

It was dark when John spotted it, after he'd been off walking over the fallow field. John had gone to look over the field to decide what he would plant there for winter crop. Potatoes maybe. Cabbage. Then he saw it and it almost took the breath from him before he had the chance to run back over the hill with the weeds and the tall grass and the bracken and the thistles pulling at his legs and his breath getting shorter as his boots sank into the earth.

Nobody knew who had put it there. John blamed Ben, because he thought Ben would do it for a laugh after all the lousy jobs John had given him. Ben denied it and blamed Butcher because Butcher had become something of a practical joker and he also drank a lot more than everyone else. Butcher denied it and said it was probably Terry and Pete, because of them all they were good with their hands and feasibly the only ones to make such a thing. But they blamed Matt and that seemed to be the most sensible option because Matt had now gone and there was surely bad blood because of it. He had left early that morning before he had a chance to hear what the group had decided the night before. Sara had gone to call him and found the room empty, the bed made and the wardrobe cleared out. There was not even a sign to suggest he had been there at all apart from a used ashtray at his bed and a copy of a book he had left on the table that had been doing the rounds called *One day in the Life of Ivan Denisovich*.

Sara was gutted as she had grown very fond of Matt and the pair had even shacked up together several times over the last few months. There was no relationship, nobody on the farm wanted that yet. But it was an understanding, which Sara felt she needed there because Joey was really the only other person she was close to. There were times when she would just knock on Matt's door at night and come in and sleep beside him with nothing physical ever taking place between them. It was just an urge to feel close to somebody and was reciprocated by Matt. So they would fall asleep in the still of the night and wake the next morning, kiss and go down for breakfast and nobody ever said a word. For days afterwards they might barely speak to one another and would just fall in with the rest of group. Then she might call to his room again. But over the weeks the time between the visits grew shorter and they both knew that one day it would have to either stop or continue as a proper relationship. Because no matter how free the heart wants to be, at some point it will grow too fond of another and see freedom as nothing but solitude. Sandra and Matt were at that point when G had gone and found what he was planting in the glasshouses. And Sara felt that although they had all voted, somehow they wouldn't follow through by sticking to the rules which Matt had maintained were there for bending anyway. But when she went and discovered Matt's disappearance the first thing she did was to rush down the corridor and kick the door to G's room almost off its hinges.

G was just up and was taken by surprise at Sara standing in the doorway with teeth clenched and her right hand rolled into a fist, her hair, usually wrapped clean in a tail, strewn across her face.

'He's gone, G, you bastard. Are you happy? You never liked him anyway, you selfish mad fucking bastard. Who do you think you are?'

John came down the corridor and put his arms around her.

'Hey, hey. It wasn't just G. It was all of us. Come on, let's go downstairs.'

But the sobbing continued as John pulled her down the stairs and G could hear his name and other names associated with it until the kitchen door closed two flights down.

G didn't have breakfast with the group that morning, he just went straight to work on the sheds until Terry and Pete arrived. First thing Terry did was to go inside and take Matt's overalls, which were hung on a nail just inside the door and walk to the end of the barnyard where they burned rubbish and wood and carcasses and anything else that needed to be got rid of, and he threw them on top of the mound of ash. By mid-morning they were all chatting loudly as ever, joined by Lofty and Ben, and nobody said a single word about Matt. And by lunchtime they were all gathered on the benches on the lawn in front of the kitchen eating sandwiches and drinking tea and nobody said a word about Matt then either. And by supper too when they were in the kitchen eating a pork meatloaf and home-baked bread and sipping cider, again nobody said a word about Matt. So it was only later that evening when John came running into the kitchen out of breath, dirty and almost disoriented that his name was mentioned for the first time and by then there was only Joey and Sara in the kitchen cleaning up.

'Where the fuck is everyone?'

Joey stared at him

'They're up in the lounge. What the hell's the matter?'

John sat and wiped the grass and seed and thorns from the bottom of his overalls with a brush.

'We just cleaned the floor, John.'

John looked down at the floor.

'Right, sorry. Something's just happened outside, that's all.'

Then he took the stairs two at a time followed by Joey and Sara and went into the lounge.

'Right, who put it there? I want to know who put it there.'

Lofty's head turned first and he leaned back in his rocking chair.

'Put what where, old boy?'

'The fuckin' thing in the field. The lower field. Who was down there today?'

Everyone looked at each other.

'Butcher, was it you?'

'Me? What did I do? Haven't been near that field for days.'

'Pete?'

'Nobody was down there today, John. Nobody is ever down there apart from Butcher and yourself. I haven't even seen that field.'

John leaned against the fireplace, sighed loudly and rubbed his eyes and took a glass from the table and poured a drink from a cider bottle.

'Okay, it's probably just a joke. But I don't like those things in the field. So whoever put it there can they just take it out.'

Jane laughed.

'John, what are you talking about? Nobody put anything anywhere.'

John turned and looked at them all individually to see if a flicker of an eye or a grin or a wink or a blush would betray someone but all he got back were blank expressions. His eyes finally landed on Ben's.

'Do you want to tell us what it is exactly, John? Any clues at all?'

'Okay. Okay. It was probably Matt then, the more I think of it. It must have been him. Some sort of joke before he left. But I'm getting rid of it, if anyone wants to help me. We don't need it anyway. Can someone help me?'

They all wanted to help John get rid of whatever it was because they were all so curious as to the mysterious object's identity. So they filed out, all of them, behind John onto the front lawn and down the pathway, through the gate and beyond the barn towards the lower field that was out of sight behind the brow of the hill. It was dusk, dampness was in the air and where the brow of the hill met the horizon the grass blurred into the sky in that purple haze that floats for just a few moments before night finally breaks.

The girls were laughing as they came over the rise, John in front looking for the first time like he actually felt out of place on his own farm, walking with Ben, Lofty, Doc and G by his side with Terry, Pete and Butcher trailing behind with Jane, Joey and Sara. Suddenly they all stopped and stared into the centre of the field that had been let lie the whole year and was overgrown waist high with almost everything that could conceivably root and take hold in the earth.

John stood still and pointed out in the field but he needn't have because there against the purple sky stood a scarecrow, arms splayed, a sackcloth face resembling sagging skin and two black eyes made from coals.

Butcher took a few steps towards it.

'What the fuck is that?'

Terry looked around him as if there might be more somewhere.

'It's a scarecrow, isn't it?'

Joey moved closer to him.

'Well, it's scaring me. Who put it there?'

Lofty sighed.

'You obviously haven't been listening to John. It was probably Matt. What do you want to do with it, old boy? Is it of any use?'

'Not here. Sure there's nothing here for crows. Anyway, I don't like them.'

John stood back from it and rubbed his chin while everyone else approached closer to the figure. The body was made from two large sticks banged together with two six-inch nails at the centre to form a cross. Over the cross an old black coat which smelled of damp was stuffed with rags and draped over the sticks, at various points secured with smaller nails. A sackcloth that bore the name of some company printed in faded ink made the face and strands of straw were pulled through the cloth to given an impression of hair. Two small pieces of coal pierced the cloth to make the eyes which where oversized and appeared hollow from a distance.

G approached the scarecrow cautiously as if it were going to make a move, then slowly rooted in the pockets of the coat, pulling out rags and tossing them aside like guts, stopping suddenly as he seemed to find something.

Ben was behind him.

'What is it, G? Is there something in there?'

G pulled his hand out slowly and opened his palm, dropping several spent shotgun cartridges on the ground beside him. Then he put his hand into the other pocket of the coat, only this time he snapped his hand back as if it was bitten. And it was Terry who then stepped forward to take his place, pulling out a dead crow, intact apart from its head which tipped to one side on a broken neck.

'Well, it wouldn't have made much of a scarecrow anyway.'

Sara put a hand to her mouth as Joey leaned over the bird that Terry had lobbed on to the ground at G's feet.

'G, was that you?'

John nudged it with his feet.

'Is that from your traps, G?'

'Possibly.'

John moved forward and put his shoulder against the torso of the scarecrow and leaned into it but there wasn't much give, so Terry and Pete joined in and rocked it forwards and backwards and sideways until they heard a crack and the body was broken in two. The scarecrow was dragged by the neck across the fields to the barn where a pyre was prepared. But before even a match was lit John insisted on going back across the fields with spades and digging up the stump of the scarecrow because he maintained that leaving roots in the ground is a sure way for something to come back. So they dug up the stump and added that to the pyre too and the whole lot went up in flames, the scarecrow, the overalls that had belonged to Matt, and barrow-loads of old leaves from the glasshouse, including leaves from Matt's plants that stank and sent clouds of smoke up into the sky that threatened to blot out the moon. By the end of the night nothing remained of that scarecrow but a mound of black ash and nobody remained outside only G, John and Butcher who stood watching the last of the embers burn out.

'Was Matt right about lighting fires, John? Is that really illegal?'

'That's bullshit, G. Been lighting fires as long as I can remember. Butcher, fetch a couple of bottles there and we'll have a drink before we go back in. Thirsty work all that burning.'

So they drank a couple of bottles each where they stood, their hands and faces covered in black soot and their clothes and hair stinking of charcoal. When they got back inside it was late and they were too tired to take showers. Instead all three cleaned up at the large ceramic sink in the kitchen, passing round a large bar of soap and watching the water turn black and run down the plug hole. John and Butcher went on ahead leaving G to do the locking up, which was a job left to one individual every night and entailed going from room to room and door to door and securing everything whether it was with a key or an old-fashioned bolt. And there were many doors and many windows and many ways in and many ways out of that house. But by then the locking up had become a drill and was done without even thinking, and no matter how tired a person was from a day's work locking up was the last order of the day.

But when G woke in the early hours of the morning the first thing he thought about was whether he had done the locking up properly. He sat up, keyed his phone beside his bed and saw that it was 4.33. He sat upright, wide awake, wondering what it was that had pulled him out of his sleep. He took a deep breath and stared around the room rubbing the film of sweat on his forehead with the back of his hand, which still smelled thinly of charcoal from the evening's burning. One great pyre they had made in the barnyard and John had stood solemn and still as the flames licked the coat of the scarecrow before finally going up in one great whoosh.

Nobody present honestly believed that Matt had put that there, but they were all still prepared to accept that it was him. Nor did anyone believe that Matt had killed a crow or taken one from the traps to place in the pocket of the scarecrow to make it look as if G had been involved. Everyone knew that Matt wouldn't hurt a fly and hated the killing of the animals, accepting it only with a heavy heart. But it was Jane and Joey who both approached G before they went inside to ask him about the scarecrow with its dead bird. G wasn't sure what to tell them. He found it difficult to explain what he had been told about the crows and how they were the devil's eyes during the day because the devil could only come out at night. And that a crow was a bad omen, a flesh-eater as well as a scavenger, which could sense death all round and on an individual before they died, even through the walls of a house. They were there to carry away the souls of the damned. But as for who had put it there G told them that he didn't know. He told them that John had spoken before about scarecrows being placed on his land and maybe it was just an old scare that people got up to on farms. Joey repeated that it had certainly scared her and for the first time since she had come down she had started to feel afraid.

And G did think more about it too. He thought about it that night as he drifted off to sleep and he knew that it was significant. As he sat there bolt upright in the bed he knew that whoever it was that had caused it was still out there. So he turned slowly and stared over at the window and at the shadows from the branches moving like limbs on the glass and he could feel his feet were tangled in the sheets as he went to step out on to the floor.

He stared at the crack at the bottom of the door for a splinter of light, a toilet flushing, someone going down for a drink of water; anything. But the house was buried in sleep and he and whoever was outside were the only bodies of consciousness at that early hour. So he moved quick and went down the corridor feeling his way along the walls to John's room at the end.

'John. John!'

John moved then jumped and leaned over to turn on the bedside light.

'Jesus Christ, G! What are you doing here?'

'Shh! Shut up for Christ's sake I don't want anyone else to wake up.'

John sat up in the bed and pushed a pillow in behind the small of his back.

'What the fuck us wrong with you? What time is it?'

'John. Listen to me, John. There's someone outside.'

John sat up further and glanced over at the window.

'John. There is someone outside.'

'I heard you the first time. Did you look? Who is it?'

'No, I didn't look! Christ, I was lying there in a sweat.'

John moved the pillow to under his head and lay back down.

'G, you're saying there's someone out there but you didn't see anyone. Now come on.'

'John, they're out there.'

'Who?'

'The brothers.'

'G, we're all a bit edgy after tonight. Go back and get some rest.'

John rolled over and pulled the duvet up to his chin, turning one last time before switching out the light.

'Did you lock up?'

'Yes.'

'You sure?'

'Yeah. Yeah, it's all locked up.'

G went back down to his own room and stared at the window with the thin curtains that acted like a screen throwing shadows and lines and shapes which fired his imagination in those small hours of the night. Only this time he was sure his imagination had nothing to do with it so he went over to the window, swept one of the curtains to the side and looked out cupping his other hand on the glass. Outside was as black as black could be, like the answer to that question he would ask his ma and da as a kid, which was if nothing existed at all, at all, at all, would it be just like the blackest of nights? And they answered that probably that was how it would be only there would be no you and no me, no love and no pain neither. So G closed the window shut and drew the curtains full and went back to sleep.

Twenty-three

When G woke again the room was flooded with light from the September morning. There was a slight chill in the air and even a glaze of frost on the window. All the signs were there that autumn was on its way and winter close behind it. Winter might not be as kind as the summer when there were long evenings and more hours to get things done. When he got downstairs most of the group were already gathered in the meeting room and Joey, Sara and Jane were discussing going out into one of the sheds which was almost finished because they wanted more space. They also had an eye on the second shed for getting some business together. John wasn't so sure.

'Like what business, Jane? Crafts or something?'

'Don't be so patronising, John. We're working on it.'

'But we need the outhouses for accommodation.'

'There are two huge spaces out there. And at the moment, I don't see who else there is to accommodate. We move out and free up some room upstairs. We're sick of sharing bathrooms. We've been talking to Terry. The first one is almost good to go. Plumbing and heating fixed, paint job and that's it.'

John shrugged and glanced over at G, who took a seat at the window in the warm spot where the sun was buttering the floor and sipped from a mug of tea with steam wafting out the top.

'It's getting cold now, Jane. You sure you're going to be happy out there? How're those buildings heated, John?'

'Oil.'

'Oil?'

G looked at Jane whose head went down on her chin, as the last conversation G and Jane had had about oil was when they were looking at a bill with figures spilling off the page. They had discussed switching to another source but that would have meant a whole other job on the house, the outhouses, everywhere, a whole new job. And that bill was for spring and summer and now autumn was knocking at the door and winter was following its path right the way up to the gate too.

'We'll manage, G. I mean, maybe we can get a generator or something.'

'And what's that going to run on?'

'Oh Jesus, G. Look, we made those sheds the priority for Terry and Pete and they've worked their asses off. They're insulated, they got a bathroom, separate bedrooms, it's what we want. We'll manage. It's one winter, how bad can it get?'

John raised an eyebrow.

'Bad. Do you not remember the last two winters, Jane? Can you imagine what it was like up here? Lost a lot of livestock even when they were in shelter. The river froze over, pipes burst and some people in these parts were stuck for weeks indoors with no way of getting out even with all-weather… anyway, we'll fix that place up nice and cosy. You'll be all right.'

'Thanks John.'

Jane left and Joey and Sara followed. G noticed what it was John was wearing on his feet and why he had been standing in the doorway the whole time.

'What's with the Wellington boots, John?'

'I need a couple of volunteers.'

'We can spare Terry.'

'We can spare you, G. And Ben too. Leave the others to get on with finishing outside. I need to build a bit of a dam.'

Ben lagged a little way behind as they walked through the knee-length grass of the paddock towards the woods with G and John. He had been happy enough sticking to the rota for the day which had him in the kitchens with Jane. Now he found himself in a pair of rubber boots heading towards the river.

'John, can I ask why we need to build a dam?'

'Fish, Ben. Fish. I'm going to teach you what it's like to be on the end of a rod. The good end that is.'

They spent the best part of the morning on the forest floor collecting logs and rocks and other material to construct the dam and by midday John was on the bank giving orders and G and Ben were in the river throwing things into place. They'd picked a good spot. Just where a small stream had joined the main river from a neighbouring field, with a large amount of bank either side at a clearing under the trees where a healthy growth of grass petered out into a bed of soft green moss near the water's edge.

'Are we done here yet? It's getting cold.'

'Just about, Ben. A few more smaller rocks in behind. We can clear away some of this growth on the bank later. Should be a grand spot to sit in. I was thinking of starting the pipe, G. Would you be on for joining me?'

'A pipe? What are you going to do, sit here with a blanket over your knees too?'

'Well I heard a fella say once that a fly fisher can never smoke a pipe. Only a bait fisher can.'

'Why's that?'

'Cos a fly fisher is always on the move. He's a hunter, looking for his prey. A bait fisher will sit and wait.'

'Well, I'd prefer to be a fly fisher then. On the move. What are you hoping to catch in here anyway? Haven't seen any sign of a fish in the last two hours.'

But John wasn't listening. He was bent over the shrubbery on the edge of the forest where it met the elevation of the paddock .

'What's up, John?'

John hesitated and G dropped the rocks he had in his hands into the water causing circles to spin out towards the bank, then he followed them and climbed up onto the soft verge and got to where John stood.

'What is it?'

John showed him the bottle he had pulled out, then walking slowly down the bank and kicking through the foliage he found several more as he cursed and kicked and each time he kicked he would find another until he had a small mound of bottles there on the bank, only they were clear glass and not brown like the ones he had in his barn. Ben waded through the water and up on to the bank to grab a bottle.

'Clean enough too.'

'The fuckers will get shot full of lead when I catch them.'

'Just kids.'

G stared up the river with the water beginning to back up behind the dam, fingers of it running over the stones like liquid silver.

'Whose land does the river flow through up beyond, John?'

John kicked the bottles together even tighter making a sound like wind chimes.

'The brothers MacMillen's old farm on Quarry Road, sure you know that, G. Why?'

'Well, because there's a million and one places around here for kids to drink. And your Gabriel's gate is locked all the time and there's a huge wall all the way round. Which means whoever got to here probably just followed the river in. Anyway, kids drink cans.'

'Cans, bottles, barrels, who cares what they drink? They drink whatever is going cheap, what's the difference?'

'What's this all about? And who are the brothers MacMillen?'

'Don't worry about it, Ben. They were neighbours, now they're gone.'

'If they're gone, why were they here drinking?'

'They weren't here, they're gone.'

'So who was hanging out down here then? Are you not worried about it?'

'Jesus, can you two give us a break? I don't know.'

Between them they gathered up the bottles in their arms and brought them back to the barn to store them in the crates next to their own brown bottles with old steel hoops. And that night after supper John requested that nobody went out to the barn for bottles of cider as they pleased, and that they should take it easy with it anyway because the supply was low. More would have to be made soon because they had a huge pick of apples from their trees and they were nice and ripe and sweet and just about ready to be pressed.

And the next morning early he took the clear glass bottles and brought them out to the other side of town to a centre that took just about every kind of rubbish you could think of, with TVs and old PCs, cardboard boxes, glass and plastic and rubber tyres, and he emptied the bottles into a great big bin that was overflowing and stinking of alcohol. Then on his way home he stopped into the hardware that was soon to close and bought the few bits and pieces that needed replacing to make the home brewed cider with his auntie's favourite recipe. He also bought more rope, a knife sharpener and a couple of good torches too.

Twenty-four

Butcher stood there with the light on. He shouldn't have switched the light on but it was too late, he stood exposed through the bare window to the person outside in the dark looking back.

After spending what was the second day on the river building up the dam, G, Ben and John had taken Pete, Terry and Butcher and grabbed a few bottles to sit for the evening at their new spot in the clearing in the woods. They built a fire that shimmered on the pool of water behind the dam. As darkness fell the pool seemed to grow deeper and the flames brighter, they pulled one bottle of cider after another out of the crate and John began telling one story after another until it was only him doing the talking and everyone else just listening and getting drunk.

'It all just goes round in one eternal circle, life on a farm like this. Animals are born, animals die. We plant the seed, we pick the crop. Sometimes we have a harvest, sometimes a whole crop fails. I've seen apple trees produce for as long as I've been coming here. You have a field that grows up to your waist and we cut it down for hay, year after year until we use the field for something else. The soil stays the same beneath our feet, replenished by the rains and dead plants and insects and animals. Always has. The only thing that changes on the farm is the people. That's the only thing. Everything else follows a natural course that you can predict and depend on, pretty much more or less. Sometimes it seems cruel that the cycle doesn't give any of these other things a different shot at life, but that's just the way it is. But the one animal that doesn't follow a natural course is people. Are you getting what I'm saying?'

Someone lobbed a bottle in the dark. It missed the crate so John leaned over unsteadily and scooped it up.

'Now there's a change coming, probably a lot sooner than I might have liked. But it's coming and it's not the type of change that we can predict or follow. Because it's got to do with some people who have never been the most pleasant in nature and I'm not quite sure what to expect. I thought it was over but it's not. What I do know is we're on our own, because there isn't anyone else out there who is ready to help us.'

John leaned on the shoulder nearest to him and stood and grabbed the shovel he had brought, which sat against a tree wedged nicely in a 'V' where two branches met and began scooping up the hot embers from the fire to throw into the pool behind the dam. Ben stood next.

'Have you got nothing to add to that, John? I mean, can you give us any more details. It's these brothers you mentioned, isn't it?'

Somebody else got to their feet.

'The brothers? Who are the brothers?'

'I'm afraid I don't have anything else, Ben. Not 'till something else happens I don't. We're going to have to sit tight.'

The embers hissed and steamed as they hit the water and a chill rose up from the river. John pulled a torch from his pocket and cut a path of light through the trees and into the paddock then led them up to the back door of the farm.

No one else was up and G had no idea what time it was when he crept up the stairs to bed and drifted into a sleep on the back of a spin caused by the amount of cider he had drunk. It must have been two or maybe three hours later when he heard it; just the one single loud crash that shattered the night like it was made of glass.

He sat up with just the hissing of silence in his ears. He could hear Ben getting up in the room next door and the creaking of floorboards, followed by his own door swinging open, the light from the corridor spilling onto his bed.

'Did you hear that, G? What the hell was it?'

After a moment of staring at each other, waiting to see if the sound would be followed by another, G swung himself out of bed and put on a sweater.

'What was it, G? What the fuck was it?'

'I don't know Ben, but it came from the meeting room right below. Come on. And quietly.'

Arriving downstairs they saw that Butcher was already there in the middle of the room looking out through a hole in the window about the size of a head, with the rest of the window veined and just about to splinter. G lunged for the light switch.

'Jesus, Butcher. You can be seen easily from outside. What's that you've got there?'

Butcher tossed something over to G.

'A rock. Like one of the rocks down at the river.'

'What were you doing down here?'

'Well, I was awake you know, couldn't sleep. And my room is overlooking the laneway and I thought I heard something outside, so I went downstairs. For another drink. To try and sleep. And just check the doors and windows.'

'Who locked up?'

They all shrugged.

'Think John locked up. But thought I'd make sure. So I checked the recreation room first, the front door, the basement door and just as I walked in here, a big rock came through the window.'

They heard feet on the stairs and turned to see John coming down two steps at a time.

'What's happened? What's that you've got, G?'

'Did you lock up?'

'Yeah.'

G tossed him the rock and nodded towards Butcher.

'Found it under the window.'

'Did you see who it was?'

Butcher hesitated.

'Did you see who it was?'

'I saw somebody. But I think there were two of them.'

John looked at the rock, turning it over in his hand. It was smooth and round and stained black from being burnt.

'Let's get down into the kitchen before any of the girls come down.'

Down in the kitchen G took the rock from John and rubbed it with his thumb, smearing the black soot.

'It looks like one of the rocks used round a fire. From down at the river or the barnyard maybe.'

Ben pulled out a stool at the counter and sat down with one leg on the floor and the other on the rung of the stool, it jittered as he spoke.

'Well, it looks like we've been watched here the last while. And don't anyone try and tell me that Matt was responsible for that scarecrow back then. It took three of us to pull it out of the ground.'

'What are you saying, Ben?'

'You know what I'm saying, Butcher. Nobody wants to admit that it wasn't Matt because we're too afraid to look at the alternative. We need answers here. Who did you see, Butcher? Out there. Let's start with that.'

Butcher took a glass and filled it with cider from the fridge.

'I just got a glimpse of the fella going back into the trees over in the corner of the garden. But I think there were two of them, like I said. The guy I saw though, was a big fucker. Jesus. Big fella.'

'I think we should call the cops. Get them up here.'

'We're not calling cops, Ben.'

'Well what else do we do, John?'

'I told you, we're on our own.'

'He's right, Ben. I've already been to the station. Don't want to know.'

'When was this, G?'

'A while back, when I went away for the night. We're on our own. Nobody wants to know.'

'Why, what happened here?'

'What happened was we didn't want to sell the land for a development that would have benefitted this town. Our neighbours did, the brothers MacMillen, and there was a dispute. We won. We kept the land and we became the bad guys.'

'And where did those brothers go, John?'

'We left them with their home and some land around it but they left. I thought one of them was dead. If not both. Nobody saw them for years, Ben, honestly. I'd no idea they were coming back here.'

'Jesus, well what do you plan on doing then?'

'We just sit tight and wait. And we sit easy. We have the advantage.'

'How in the name of Jesus do we have an advantage? Butcher almost had his skull cracked open with a rock.'

'Well, do you remember tonight we were talking about hunting? Well, a lot of hunters underestimate the intelligence of their prey. The reason we do nothing, is because we're unafraid. Because we all know every inch of this place and we can outwit whoever comes in here.'

'Sure. So who's going to help us? Your wooden angel on the gate?'

G pulled out the stool beside Ben and sat next to him.

'Keep your voice down, Ben. Now relax, it's going to be fine.'

'So what are we really talking about here?'

G looked over at John.

'About defending ourselves and our right to live here. What have we got, John?'

'The shotguns. Three we can use.'

'For God's sake, I mean, it was only a rock, John.'

'What do you think we should use, Ben? Pitchforks?'

'I don't think we should be using anything.'

'So we just quit then. Like everyone else. Just walk away. This is my land, Ben. Our land now. There are laws to deal with trespassers and I've licences for those guns. If we're under threat we're entitled to use them. Trust me.'

Ben rubbed his eyes hard then ran his hands through hair which hadn't been cut in months or even washed properly for that matter, and it was growing down over a face that was tanned and windblown and like most of the guys on the farm hardly ever clean-shaven either. He had lost some weight, looking the better for it, but his skin had seemed to age somewhat, lines shooting out at right angles from his eyes and across his forehead in crevasses. In fact, they had all become dishevelled, even the girls. Not that any of them were concerned.

There was never any need to dress up because who was there to impress only each other? They all knew each other well enough by now and had been too busy with the workload to be concerned with vanity.

Ben leaned across Butcher and took the cider bottle and swigged from the neck.

'I'm tired guys. Is anyone else tired? I mean, physically and mentally tired. We've done nothing but work for the last couple of months, fourteen hours a day almost. I'm tired and I think it's beginning to take its toll. It could have been a couple of kids out there messing. For God's sake, I'm beginning to think we're developing cabin fever in this place. We need to get a grip. That's what I think.'

John nodded.

'Maybe you're right, Ben. I think we all need a bit of a break soon, to be honest. Take a week or two off. The lot of us. Head home and chill out then come back end of autumn. There is a lot of work to do first, to get ready for winter. But if we knuckle down we can get through it and give ourselves some time. What do you say to that, G?'

'Autumn. Hard to believe it's nearly autumn already. Where does the time go? Butcher. Do you need a break?'

'Well, we've been working hard, like Ben said. Might do us all some good.'

John slapped Butcher gently on the back.

'Well, we'll put it to the rest of them in a couple of weeks. See what they say. Let's get back to bed. Come on Ben, get some sleep, mate.'

Ben stalled.

'And the window? Butcher, what are you going to say? You were there first.'

Butcher shrugged.

'Say one of G's crows flew into it.'

John picked up the rock from the counter and rolled around in his hands.

'We'll just tell them I broke it moving some furniture. I'll make sure I'm up early enough. But not a word to anyone about this for the time being.'

Before they left John opened the back door of the kitchen and looked out. But there was nothing moving out there. Not a stir. So he took a few steps down towards the barnyard and lobbed the rock over towards the back wall where the fires were made. It rolled and toppled, then came to a stop.

Twenty-five

Autumn colours of browns and golds and the grass damp with morning rain; layers of mist creeping across the fields in the evening and rust red leaves forming rugs on the forest floor; moss on the laneway the colour of emerald and branches of trees stripped and gaunt; night coming tumbling over the hills earlier each day and the warmth of the sun fading on the backs of the people toiling in the earth —Autumn is like a rake and clears the path for winter which levels all things under a cold stark layer of white. October.

A lot of killing had to be done. There was a cow, the second pig, several broiler chickens and a couple of sheep. John didn't want to kill that particular cow. He'd had that cow for quite some time and recalled G had given it a name. But it was necessary now that winter was almost upon them and anyway he still had three and could purchase new stock come spring. But killing the cow wasn't easy. Even Butcher looked shaken at the end of it. And the girls were upset. Joey had said that cows, even more so than pigs, could sense death when it came.

John had to sit with the girls that evening for some time trying to get them to accept that all animals sense death, even humans, and that it was the strongest sense that one has. But death in nature was something that they had all been growing close to and that was why he had forced them all to partake in that long week of slaughter when the barnyard ran red with blood and the group's clothes were stained dark. The smell took days to leave them and the huge heap of discarded flesh and bone was plundered by crows night and day, not even the fire burned quick enough to keep them away.

John did everything to burn the carcasses that built up. He soaked them in diesel and added old broken furniture and rubbish that they had found in the attic: old clothes belonging to his uncle and his aunt, dungarees and long dresses, books that were yellowed and had their backs broken, tea chests full of old costume jewellery that nobody would ever want. John had wanted to hang on to it all, or at least as much as he could, but he was only being sentimental and he couldn't preach sentimentality after what he had been telling everyone. It was hard for him that week. He felt the loss of the animals too. And he felt the loss of his uncle and his aunt, both of whom had been like parents to him as he grew up. Each object he burned had a story. Each item of clothing a scent of his uncle or aunt, even after all those years. But he knew he had to clear them all out as the farm was now home to new people and life had to go on.

The fire was large and thick with plumes of black smoke, blacker than the night sky and blacker than the crows that had flown around it before the flames licked the rotten flesh from the animals' corpses. It was blacker than the eyes of coal that were stuck to the face of the scarecrow. It burned and hissed and popped into the early hours of the morning when some of the group volunteered to shovel the remaining ash into barrows and wheel it down into the river where it was swept away by the waters and out into the sea. By the end of that week, not a trace remained of the cow, the pig, nor any of the chickens. Not a trace remained even of the personal belongings of John's uncle and aunt who were long dead anyway, buried in the earth.

As strong as G had shown himself to be during the slaughter, towards the end of the week he appeared almost terrified, relaxing only when the fire had burnt out and the crows had gone beyond the hills to wherever it was that they all came from. Few of the group spoke much, most withdrew to their own rooms in the evening or sat quietly downstairs in small groups. Once it was done and the larders and freezers were stocked full for the winter things settled a bit, but it had been tough, and John in particular noticed it had taken its toll on G. But he said nothing. Instead one morning he called him early and took him to the river fishing, and a crisp and dry morning it was as the grass in the paddock crunched from frost beneath their feet as they walked, John talked and talked and by the time they reached the river G's mood had turned.

John knew G had grown to like fishing, even if he insisted he would have preferred fly-fishing. There were many times he would just throw the fish he caught back into the water saying they were too small and that it wasn't fair and he'd recognise them again when they were bigger. John could have fed two mouths with the ones G had caught, but he didn't say anything to G. He knew G just liked the idea of fishing, sitting by the river and letting time slip by.

When they reached the bank John threw a blanket on the ground and opened his box of tackle, taking a worm between thumb and forefinger and squeezing it onto his hook before casting the line into the river. It hit the water with a plop and he sat back, pouring two mugs of coffee from a flask.

'These brothers we're talking about, G, you saw where they lived, outside the town off the Quarry Road. When I stayed here first during the summers as a kid, me and the lads used to have dares to see who could get closest to the house. God, I used to shit myself, G. We'd take it in turns to creep down the lane and see who could get the furthest.

'The lane was quite long and narrow with thick hedge either side and in the summers it was nothing but dust. I think they used to hear us coming down that lane, our boots scrunching the stone and dust and kicking up a trail, no matter how quiet we thought we were. Just when we were near the house, out one of them would come. He'd just stand there in the doorway and stare out and we'd run like the blazes.

'But one day, I got right into the garden and there was the big guy, splitting logs. I timed my footsteps so they hit the ground as he hit the logs. I thought I was being clever. He never said anything when he saw me behind a tree. Just turned with the axe in the air and stared at me. I couldn't move. Eventually, he just brought the axe down on the log and I ran out down the lane like the hammers of hell. His name was Heiney. We had all sorts of nicknames for him, like Hulk Heiney, all that.'

'And you've never spoken to him?'

John shook his head.

'My uncle had a bad time with him. They were constantly at war with him, even before the land dispute. But we didn't treat them too bad. We let them stay where they were. Do you know the amount of people who were being tossed off their land G, during the whole boom? And not just by landowners, but by councils. At least we had some honour. But it wasn't enough. And I'm convinced that some of the things that went on around the farm afterwards – sheep slaughtered, machinery sabotaged, fires started and scarecrows appearing overnight – they were down to them. Even though everyone said they were gone.'

'But you never saw them again? When these things were going on.'

'Let's say I felt him. The older one. He's doing the same thing to us as he did to my uncle. That's what killed him in the end, I'd say. Down in the far field that we've left fallow. Where the scarecrow was. I found him. Lying there dead. G, I'm getting tired of death in this place.'

G lobbed a large stone into the centre of the pool behind the dam suddenly, the splash causing John to fall back from the log he was sitting on.

'Did you see that rock, John?'

'Great. You've scared the fish away now.'

'When we dammed up the river here with the rocks, what did we do?'

'What do you mean, what did we do? We dammed the river, like you said.'

'Right. So it would be like shooting fish in a barrel, if we were using guns instead of rods.'

'Right.'

'Well, that's what we've become here, John. I just never saw it until now.'

'What are you talking about?'

'We said that we were doing this to know how it really feels to have the freedom to live by our own means. But I worry that all we've done is build ourselves a great big dam. You said yourself, if it weren't for those rocks, the fish would be swimming on to wherever they were meant to go.'

'Ah, Jesus, G.'

'I just have a bad feeling. These brothers, why are they here? Think about it for a moment, John.'

John stood and went to the edge of the river and looked into the pool that had been created since they damned it up a few weeks back. They had caught many fish in there while others had slipped through, the small ones through the gaps and the larger ones by jumping over the rocks. But there were plenty of fish in there now, shadows in the deep pool, twisting and turning, not sure which direction to take, the current behind too strong and the wall of rock in front too great. They would remain there until caught, spinning endlessly with no direction, or they would hope to get big enough to jump to freedom. But time wouldn't be on their side to allow that.

'I don't know. They've always been here.'

G nodded.

'That's what worries me.'

John saw his rod tremble and a circle appear in the pool where the line cut in, so he pulled it back and wound the reel, bringing up a large fish. He struggled with it for a moment as its head went back into the water then wound the reel a bit further, this time bringing the rod back over his shoulder pulling the fish in towards the bank. Then he grabbed the net and scooped up the fish using the experience and dexterity he had honed over the years, removing the hook from the fish's mouth with one squeeze and holding it up for G to see.

'Throw it back, let's go.'

'Throw it back? Are you joking me?'

G walked away along the path that had been beaten down by their constant comings and goings out through the trees towards the paddock. John looked at the fish in the net as it flipped over from one side to the other, its mouth agape and its scales shining as the water rolled off its body. Then he threw it back.

'Did I tell you I bought a horse?'

'No. Did you tell Jane?'

John was a few paces behind G, his breath steaming in the autumn air.

'What do I need to tell Jane for?'

'Because she is in charge of accounts, John. We agreed. No more investments without approval and any new purchases have to help cut costs.'

'This will cut costs.'

'How?'

'Have you never heard of a horse power?'

'Are you being serious?'

'Of course I'm being serious. Butcher is picking her up this morning.'

'Which is why you dragged me down to the river.'

'Well, didn't want to discuss it over breakfast. It's a surprise.'

'Hell of a surprise.'

'G, we've been spending a lot of money on fuel. Energy bills are going up. That tractor is costing a fortune to run and a horse can do a lot of work here. We got plenty of vintage machinery like rollers and ploughs that can be cleaned up. It's cheaper, greener, she can tackle tricky terrain like some of those fields beyond and we can use the manure. We're not using enough of the land we've got to warrant using a tractor all the time and we can't keep doing the smaller allotments by hand. Besides, a horse is better company when you're out on your own all day.'

'Whatever you say, John. We haven't made a cent this year, all we've done is spend.'

'We've got the farm back in shape, G. That was the target. Next year we can look at the business end of it.'

They reached the house and kicked their boots against the wall before going in the back door to the kitchen to make tea in a large pot and fry some eggs on a pan over the stove.

'Could have had nice fried fish if you hadn't made me throw it back.'

'I never made you.'

'Well you caught me out in a moment of compassion.'

G heard the sound of voices coming down the stairs and one by one they descended, Doc first, who stood on his toes and peered over John's shoulder .

'You making eggs?'

'For G and myself only.'

John glanced at the notice board on the wall below the clock to the roster drawn up on a spreadsheet.

'It's Butcher and Jane this week on the roster.'

'I'm starved.'

G passed the eggs, which were in a large bowl, over to John, who sighed and broke a few more as the rest of the group came in, some in long sweaters complaining about the cold, rubbing their hands and peering over John's shoulder too.

'That all we got? Eggs?'

John looked behind him at the voice which belonged to Terry.

'I'm not even on the roster. Now put on some toast if you want.'

'Who is then?'

'Butcher.'

Jane came in and took the bread from the counter.

'And me? Where is Butcher?'

'He's gone to pick something up for me. For us.'

Jane looked over at G who smiled.

'What's he getting, John?'

'It's a surprise, Jane.'

As the eggs began to spit in the pan there was a crunch of gravel on the lane outside and a van pulled up with a man driving, Butcher in the passenger seat and in tow was a horse box that wobbled from side to side. The van stopped and the horsebox lurched. Butcher and the man both climbed out and went round to the back of it. Butcher stood by as the man opened it and began pulling a beast out by the rope, shouting and hollering at the same time. The head came first and it shook from one side to the next, just like the fish John had on the end of his line, so the man yanked some more and hollered even louder then finally the front legs followed.

Doc was over John's shoulder again and behind him stood the rest of the group watching the spectacle unfold in front of the house.

'Jesus. What did you get this time? This our next meal?'

'A horse, Doc. A horse. Someone look after them eggs.'

John went out the back door and was followed by Jane, Joey and Sara just as the rest of the horse was coaxed out of the box, a large beast of a draught horse, maple brown with white spots either side and tufts of hair covering the hooves. Once out of the box it shook itself for a moment then settled down and raised its head. If horses had a smile then this one looked like it did. John beamed.

'Of all the animals, horses are the most splendid.'

The girls approached and began to pet it as Butcher shared a few words with the man who then drove away down the lane. Jane put her hand on the horse's head and began stroking it behind the ears.

'What are we going to call him?'

John laughed.

'It's a she.'

'Her then.'

'I'll let you girls decide.'

'We'll call her Dipsy.'

John looked at Jane who was continuing to stroke the horse behind the ears then glanced at Sara and Joey and shrugged.

'Any objections?'

Jane turned to look at them.

'Sara?'

'Fine by me.'

'Joey?'

'I would have went for… it's fine by me too.'

John nodded.

'Dipsy it is.'

So John took Dipsy by the rope and led him around to the barnyard where at the back lay a stable full of hay. He got a brush and a pot of paint that Terry and Pete had been using at the outhouses and put in big white letters on the staple door, 'DIPSY.'

Twenty-six

The dam, which had been built good and sturdy with plenty of logs for support and enough stone and gravel and rock to hold the force of the river, had been completely destroyed only the day after John and G had been down there fishing. There had been no high winds or floods to cause a surge of water so the damage could only have been done by hand, and even at that it would have taken time and it would have taken someone with the strength of several men to tear it apart and scatter the bulk of it down river.

'It's time to take that break, G.'

'Are we done with the harvesting? Can we manage?'

'As good as. Bit more to do but, that's feasibly all we can manage now till after winter anyway.'

G took some clothes out of his wardrobe, found the fleece he had been looking for and pulled it on over his sweater. It was early and it was cold and condensation covered the windows in his bedroom. John stood beside G with his hands on his hips, a hat and coat still on then he wiped his nose with his forearm and sniffled.

'So what do you think? Should we take the break or not?'

'What happened exactly?'

'Don't know. The fuckin' dam is just gone. There yesterday morning, gone this morning. Just like that. Rocks are all over the place. The river is running along through it and our pool is gone. At least your fish can move on to wherever they were going.'

'Okay. Let's decide to call a two-week break from the end of this week. We'll tell them at the meeting this evening. Get them back by the start of November and we can knuckle down to the winter. It's a good time for a break anyway. While they're gone maybe we can sort this shit out ourselves. Do you need anyone else to stay?'

John shook his head and wiped at his nose again which was running a bit on to his top lip.

'No. Just you and me. Unless you want to go too.'

'Me? No. Nowhere else I want to be.'

The meeting that evening didn't go as well as it should have since nobody was very keen on taking a break, and the argument was put that if they wanted to take a break, why couldn't they all just chill out where they were? But John was insistent. He wanted to clear the farm he said. He had a lot of things to do himself and there would be chemicals and mess and he'd rather just have the place to himself for a couple of weeks to finish it all off, tidy up and get the plumbing and the heating all prepped for winter because he was sure it was going to be another cold one.

Ben wasn't convinced. Most of the farm was kept free from chemicals so they could apply for their organic certification, and wasn't that why they all had to work so hard. But at least he had the sense to stay quiet during the meeting. Eventually it was put to a vote just like it always was and by a narrow margin it was accepted that they would go.

Jane was reluctant. She spoke with G later that evening outside on one of the benches down near the woods as the air was beginning to crackle with an oncoming frost, G had got up close beside her and put an arm around her to keep her warm as she dragged on a cigarette and blew thin wisps of smoke out the side of her mouth as she spoke.

'What's all this about taking a break, G?'

'We've a few things to sort out here and it's best if it's quiet while we're doing it.'

Jane sighed loudly then flicked the cigarette butt into the grass where it hissed and burned out.

'Like what? Stuff in the town? There's nobody gives a shit down there now.'

'Well, yes and no. I'm not saying anything more about it, Jane. So there's no point asking me.'

Jane leaned her head on G's shoulder.

'Do you want me to come back?'

G held her tightly and looked out across the farm and the fields rolling into one another and the large October moon rising up behind the hills.

'Of course I want you to come back.'

'I mean it, G. Do you want me to come back? If you don't, I'm not coming. Do you understand? I'm not going to stay here any longer if we're not together. We're either together or apart. But not apart together, if that makes sense.'

'It makes sense.'

'Well, then?'

'I want you to come back, Jane.'

'Okay. Now, are you going to come to bed with me?'

G laughed and shook his head then he took Jane's hand and squeezed it gently allowing their fingers intertwine like strands of ivy.

'Have we got any wine left in there?'

'Sure. Loads.'

'Let's get a bottle and bring it upstairs. You and me. Actually, let's get a few bottles and not come down until Sunday. I'm not doing another thing on this bloody farm for the next few days.'

Jane laughed.

'What are we going to eat?'

'Wine.'

Jane was beside him in the bed. G had awoken late. He looked at her, lying there asleep, and realised that he had missed her a lot over the last few months. Even though she was there all the time, in the same house, in the same rooms every evening, in the same places every day. He thought that eventually they would drift apart and become used to simply being around each other. But it doesn't work like that. The spark was still very much there and it didn't take much for it to return. He loved her.

He looked at his watch. It was already lunchtime and the farm was quiet. He climbed out of bed and went down the corridor. The rooms were all empty. Downstairs, the rooms were empty too, the only sound coming from a radio in the kitchen but when he went down nobody was there. On the kitchen table was a note from John. He didn't want to disturb him and had left to give some of the people a lift out. He didn't expect to be back until later that evening.

'Shit.'

Jane arrived in the kitchen wearing one of G's sweaters looking sleepy and needing some coffee.

'They've all gone, Jane.'

'Oh, no. Why didn't they wait? What time is it now?'

'It's after two. I suppose they didn't want to disturb us. We've been hiding up there the last few days.'

Jane laughed and shrugged and put her arms around G from behind and gave a him a long hug.

'What do you want to do?'

'Well, go, I suppose. I can get a bus out of here and catch a train later. There's one tonight.'

'Why don't you just wait until the morning?'

'Nah. I'm going now, G. I'll be fine. I'll stroll down later.'

They made coffee and fried up some bacon with eggs and tomato and a few sides of toast and G squeezed oranges to make juice. When they had finished G pulled on some overalls and went to the outhouses while Jane went upstairs to pack.

Outside a hard crust of frost lingered, turning the ground to steel. G examined the walls of the outhouses, running his hands over the surface which had been plastered smooth and whitewashed. In front lay the scaffolding, which had been dismantled and propped against a large barrel of water they had used for cleaning brushes but was frozen now with a top of ice. G gave it a kick but the sound was hollow. He pushed open the door of the first outhouse which was almost done, only the walls inside needing one more layer of paint.

It grew dull by early evening and clouds rolled in promising cold rain or even sleet or hail. G was warming up from painting but his hands were still cold and he had to stop occasionally and rub them together, standing back to admire what had once been shacks ravaged by rodents and spiders with windows thick from cobwebs but had become spacious dwellings, partitioned into separate rooms with a small communal area and bathroom ready for the final plumbing. He felt the doorway darken and turned to see Jane standing with her hand on the top of the frame, leaning in from outside.

'You going already?'

'I gotta go. There's a bus in about forty minutes. Don't worry, you stay here.'

'Just give me a minute, I'll change and go down with you. It's getting dark and it's probably going to rain. Come on.'

Jane came over to him, planted a long kiss on his mouth and placed the palm of her hand on his cheek. Then she went back to the door and turned looking directly at him.

'G, I'm not coming back.'

'What do you mean? I thought we decided all this.'

'We did, but I've changed my mind. My Visa came through. I just checked. I'm going to use it.'

'For where?'

'Canada. I've friends over there, G. You should come too, really. Let's both go. There's no future here anymore. Do you not see that?'

'No future? You mean here, at our farm?' G's mouth stayed open in disbelief.

'I mean at this farm and I mean in this country, G. We got to get out.'

'Out? What do you mean out? After all the work we've put into this place? It's finished. It's done.'

'Well, I'm not so sure about it anymore. It doesn't feel

right. I'm not even enjoying it now. It's been getting real cold, the nights are longer and longer and I'm always hungry —I've a bad feeling about the place now, G. I want to go somewhere with a bit more hope.'

'Hope? And what about the last few days we just had?'

'So they were the last few days, G. It was an episode, a period of time, the way you always look at things. But you never join the dots to look at the bigger picture. I was here for months and you were miles away.'

G threw the brush on the concrete floor, it rolled over once and gathered grit.

'I was busy. Jesus! I can't just walk away from all this now, Jane. I just can't.'

Jane grabbed her bag and raised it from the ground slightly.

'I know. Look, I'll message you. Let you know how I'm getting on. You can find me on Facebook. I'll stay on it, I promise.'

'There's nothing I can say?'

Jane shook her head.

G stood in the doorway and watched her go up the gravel path, through the gate and around the corner onto the lawn until he could see her no more. He could just hear her footsteps on the laneway, then nothing but the wind across the tops of the trees carrying rain, and emptiness too.

He finished up the wall he was working on then went back inside as a swirl of rain and sleet came across the fields, looking like a plague of locusts. He lit the fire in the lounge and fried up a couple of pork chops, put them on slices of bread and butter, grabbed a few bottles of cider from the larder and carried the lot on a tray to sit in front of the flames by himself, eating and drinking and rocking in the chair normally reserved for Lofty.

Apart from the gentle creak of the chair and the crunch of wood on wood beneath the legs there was not a sound to be heard in a house usually filled with music and laughter or crying or shouting or singing and dancing. Now there was nothing. Jane, Joey, Sara, John, Ben, Lofty, Terry, Butcher, Doc and Pete; he missed them all already.

G stood and went to the window to pull the heavy curtains over and keep in the heat from the fire which was warming up the room nicely. The cider was doing its job too, warming him from the inside. He took one last glance through the window as darkness fell and sleet spat on the glass. He could make out the trees across the lawn and the limbs moving up and down in the wind. For a moment the thought occurred to him that MacMillen was in there watching; watching with his brother by his side. But he took a long swig of cider and felt his eyes water; that stopped his thoughts from developing any further on the matter. Then he pulled the last bit of curtain across and sat back down to wait for John.

Twenty-seven

It was the day of All Hallows, November 1, when the first sighting of the brothers MacMillen was recorded on the farm. They had celebrated Halloween on their return the night before with the largest bonfire they'd ever had in the barnyard and it was composed of all the things that G and John had been gathering while the group were away. They had combed the floor of the forest and collected dead wood and barrows of leaves, branches that had been blown down in high winds and slabs of fungus growing at the base of trees that made perfect tinder. They cleared out the barn and found old tyres from tractors and harvesters and trucks, with holes so big you could climb through them; fence posts wrapped with wire that glowed red for hours after they burned; compost and manure and layers of flattened hay from Dipsy's stable; old furniture, empty paint tins, clothes and boots and shoes. And to crown the fire they had an effigy of a banker, which was G's idea, and they had found an old suit and stuffed that with straw after making a 'T' shape with two planks of wood. John had an old monopoly game so they stuffed the pockets of the suit with money that and John even wanted to burn the old loan agreement too but G said he should keep it just in case. When the fire licked the trousers of the banker there was a loud cheer from the party and an even bigger one when it was engulfed in flames and toppled head first into the main body of the blaze, which was so hot they had to sit several yards back from it.

Nobody rose the next day until well after lunch, for it was a bitterly cold day and so dull and dark and grey it was as if there was no day at all and it was merely a thin layer over night which had never budged. A few had gone out to the barnyard to help clear the mess of ash and deformed objects, twisted metal, buckled nails and blackened wire, which lay in a heap in a great circle at the centre of the yard. John was worried that Dipsy would injure herself out there and insisted it was cleaned up properly so nothing remained but scorched earth. But apart from that, no other work was done that day and few spoke through their hangovers, praying that sleep would come early that night.

But it didn't come early for everyone. Not for Joey who had been sitting in the common room of the outhouse after she had surrendered to the insomnia that had come with her refusal to drink at all that night. Most of the others, including Sara, had drank a good deal of red wine and were in the middle of a perfect slumber, but well after midnight Joey was still up hoping to read herself to sleep with just a small lamp on behind her shoulder. She heard a sound first out in the yard, like something had toppled over, then she heard Dipsy neigh and kick out in the stable so she went to the window and parted the curtain to look out, but instead of looking into the night she looked into the eyes of a stranger who blinked just once. His eyes were the eyes of a goat, she said, with a soft yellow on the edges and dark pupils like the blackest of stone.

Her screams woke Sara immediately and they called John on his mobile, and he woke G and they both ran to the outhouses but saw nobody on the way. Joey and Sara had to move back inside that night and the next morning over breakfast the subject was raised with Doc who was wondering whether she hadn't just imagined things after all the alcohol and possibly drugs from the night before.

'I didn't imagine it, Doc.'

'But your lamp was on behind you. You sure it wasn't just a reflection in the glass or something?'

'No. I cupped my hands over the glass and I stared right into this guy's eyes. I won't ever forget it.'

'Who might it have been, John. Any ideas?'

John shrugged and cut a slice of toast down the middle.

'Could have been anyone, Doc. Look, break-ins have shot up. My guess is they might have been casing the place the last few days with just myself and G here. Probably didn't expect anyone to be in the outhouse. The main thing is everyone is safe and nothing is stolen. We just need to be on our guard. You should probably move back in for a while though, Joey.'

'We're not moving back in. That's our new home.'

Terry pushed some dishes aside on the table and leaned forward on his elbows.

'You said they, John. How do you know it was they? Joey said she only saw one bloke.'

'Whatever, they… meaning, in general. Burglars, thieves, whatever you want to call them,' said John, clearly flustered.

'So you've no idea who it might have been?'

'None, Terry. Look, it's the first time it's happened.'

Pete butted in.

'What time was this anyway, Joey?'

'After twelve some time.'

'Then you came in here?'

'Yeah, we both came in with John and G, why?'

Pete smiled and shook his head.

'Have you been out there this morning yet?'

'No, it's like eight o'clock, we're all just up.'

'What are you saying, Pete?'

'I'm saying, John, that we don't know if he – or they

– went away at all last night. I'm saying we should go out and check outside.'

How nobody had heard what had happened was the biggest mystery. For whoever it was that took the horse from the stable must have pulled back the large metal bolts, which would have sounded like a hammer landing hard on an anvil. Then the horse itself would have made a racket being dragged out into the night by strangers, probably by torchlight and probably on the end of a rope, kicking and rearing up in the struggle. Then it would have had to have been tied down somehow on the earth which had been scorched from the bonfire the previous night, probably to several stakes in the ground, before it was soaked in accelerant of some sort, petrol most likely, and set alight to burn and become as black as it was, a twisted carcass with no skin whatsoever, barely any bone apart from jaws held agape in that last whine of pain to reveal the brute's teeth.

They all just stood there, silent for a long moment, disgusted, shaken.

'Jesus Christ. The poor thing. I just hope she was shot first. Poor thing.'

G shook his head.

'We would have heard it, John. Someone would have heard a gunshot.'

'We would have heard this poor thing. We should have heard it. How did we not hear it?'

John looked around at the others who had not yet ran back inside. Butcher, Doc and Terry.

'We've got to bury the rest of this horse. Can you give me a hand? I know it's not pleasant.'

They nodded, but G had turned and was looking over towards the stables. Then he looked at John.

What is it, G. What are you looking at me like that for?'

'The dogs, John. The sheepdogs. They're very quiet.'

'Oh, no. Not my dogs too.'

There were tears in John's eyes but they could have been caused by the wind which had ice in it, and he pulled his hat down over them and went into the barn to fetch a couple of shovels and the wheelbarrow and together they dug up the remains of the horse which was partly stuck fast to the earth and loaded it into the barrow to be wheeled down near the river and buried. The dogs were nowhere to be seen, John reckoned they had been taken or cast away somewhere, dead.

By the time they had completed the task it was nearing nightfall. Nothing remained of the horse but a black outline on the floor of the yard and the scent in the stable, which John vowed to disinfect and clean out first thing in the morning.

Twenty-eight

November had stripped everything bare. The trees were thin and gaunt and the branches shook and bent over in cold north winds. Weeks of frost had chewed away any colour from the fields and only the stalks of what had once bloomed in summer broke the monotony of frozen clay. Ice formed wherever it could get a hold – animal tracks, footprints, small craters and the furrows of fields – and it got into the bones of every animal exposed, including the people on the farm.

Finding the heart to do any kind of manual labour was hard. Nothing seemed to keep the cold from penetrating the winter clothes. Even the house rarely seemed to warm up. With the central heating on a timer to save the oil that was running dangerously low, the only rooms warm enough to sit in were the kitchen, where the stove always burned, and the lounge, with its open fire glowing from late afternoon until the small hours of the morning. The group huddled there in front of the flames for as long as they could remain awake, crawling into cold beds after midnight with socks and sweaters on, listening to the walls creak, the pipes, the

TOM GALVIN

foundations of the building, the roof and the timber joists, all groan and contract as temperatures dropped.

It had been over a week since Joey had sighted the man at the window and neither she nor Sara had gone back out to the new building, sleeping in their old room together instead. Although nothing had happened since, the subject of the horse being burned alive and the dogs disappearing had refused to go away. They expected the dogs to turn up, dead and frozen in a ditch somewhere. They expected more animals to vanish. They expected more fires or vandalism or for some of the farm machinery to be stolen. And they expected to hear something from someone about why they were being targeted, some conditions and some demands at least. But nothing came. And there were many who felt the project was doomed and could never recover, not just from the previous incidents but from the doubt and fear that had crept in.

Whispers circulated that people were making plans to leave, that John or G or both had been lying about what they knew and once winter was done, they would all pack up and abandon the farm. It was going to take just one more incident, one more push. But nobody expected it to end the way it did.

The names that morning were handwritten when they were usually typed up. John was getting sloppy or

269

lazy or plain disinterested, or maybe too occupied with whatever was haunting the place. He'd scrawled a list on a sheet of paper quickly before breakfast and left it on the kitchen table. Big bold letters in black ink and people stared at them for longer than it took to actually read them.

Pete and Sara: sewing garlic. Joey: clearing out the greenhouses. Terry and John: gathering and chopping firewood. Ben and Butcher: packaging seed. Lofty and G: picking potatoes and storage.

By mid-afternoon so many had complained their fingers were ravaged by the cold that John allowed them to go back inside and someone mentioned lighting the fire and making a large stew for supper. So that was settled, and they returned early and kicked off their boots at the back door to the kitchen. Once inside they rubbed their feet and peeled off hats and coats and layers beneath and lit the fire up in the lounge while a few volunteers helped Doc and Sara, who were on the roster that day, to prepare and make up a stew of beef, plenty of vegetables and a good lashing of red wine that filled the air with the scent of warmth.

Joey had opted to stay in the glasshouses, which were sheltered and conditions were more preferable to work in. Besides, she was carrying out a task that was long overdue, stripping the place of the plants which had given up their fruit all summer and into autumn and lay bare and draped on the wires which ran the length of the glasshouses.

But as dusk approached so too did a cold bank of mist and there was little of the faded yellow sun left to keep the place warm and so she also succumbed to the elements and left the stripped plants in a heap in the centre. She walked briskly up through the paddock hugging herself and pulling her hat down low over her face and ears.

It was then she noticed something, out in the first field where the few cattle stood still like tombstones, their figures all distorted and starting to swirl in the mist. She stopped and stared and gave a quick mental count of how many were stood there and how many John had; the number didn't tally. She blinked and tried to focus. Droplets of mist floated on to her eyelids and she blinked again and wiped her eyes with her gloved fingers as two of the figures moved and joined each other as if becoming one, then quickly began to approach her.

She took a few steps back feeling the frost give under her feet. Then she turned and moved quickly but they moved quicker so she ran across the paddock, seeing her breath cloud in front of her as she used the small light on the side wall of the farmhouse near the kitchen door as a pinpoint, cursing G as she stumbled for never getting proper lights out there as he had promised to do months ago.

The frozen grass under her feet turned to frozen gravel as she hit the path and she could see through the kitchen window the figures of Doc, G, Sara and John who could hear nothing of her approach. She was so close she could smell the wine in the stew and see the steam pour out through the vent over the kitchen windows. So she shouted and Sara looked out, but could see little as darkness was falling and Joey caught only an image of herself in the glass.

She shouted again. This time Sara heard and opened the kitchen door and Joey came and stood just inside, silent for a moment, her arms by her sides, heaving as she got her breath back. Then she turned, slammed the door and drew the bolts across at the top then kicked the one at the bottom several times over.

'He's back. And there's two of them.'

She grabbed hold of Doc who was nearest to her and stared up at the windows over the ceramic sink waiting for them to darken with the faces of whoever was out there. Doc looked up. So did Sara and G and John. For a moment not a word was said and the only sound came from the hissing of damp logs burning in the stove and the tap running cold on to a cauldron of potatoes waiting to be peeled. John leaned into the sink and turned the tap off, glancing up at the windows again where the dusk was pulling the night down behind it.

'Everyone up into the lounge. Everyone. Ring the bell and get everyone in together.'

G led the way up the stairs. As he reached the top the clock in the hall chimed seven times, he waited until it stopped then he grabbed hold of the leather thong dangling from the centre of the bell and rang it good and loud for a long time, longer even than it had taken the clock to chime seven times.

People appeared from various doors and at the top of the stairs, some with blankets over them, yawning and stretching and figuring dinner was ready, but when they saw G frantically ringing the bell and the other four standing all solemn in the hallway their expressions changed and they knew this had nothing to do with dinner.

When everyone had gathered in the hallway John stood halfway up the stairs, but before he had a chance to say anything Joey raised a hand.

'I just want to get out of here, John.'

John looked at the front door which he had bolted fast then he scanned the other faces which were blank and confused.

'You can't go now, Joey. Nobody can go now. They're here.'

Terry looked up at him.

'Who's here?'

'The brothers.'

'Who the hell are the brothers?'

'The brothers MacMillen. They've come back now. Finally they've shown themselves.'

'What are they here for?'

'For me. For us.'

'So is that for you or for us, John?'

'We'll have to see, Terry. Do you want to walk out there and find out?'

Doc had an arm on Joey's shoulder, he pulled her tighter and closer to him.

'Are these the same brothers who killed the horse, John?'

'That's right, Doc.'

'And took your dogs?'

'That's right.'

'And destroyed the dam?'

'That too.'

'And planted the scarecrow?'

John nodded.

'And a lot more they've done besides, Doc.'

'So why have you waited until now to tell us?'

'Because it's only now they've shown themselves. I didn't know where they were. Nobody did. They should have been gone.'

'But you kept us in the dark this long?'

'You were better off in the dark. Believe me.'

'So can we call the police? Can we call someone down the town?'

G looked over at Doc.

'There's no point calling the police, Doc. I already spoke to them. They're not going to help. Nobody will. I asked. I asked everyone. We're on our own.'

'Jesus. So you knew this was coming too? And you did nothing to try and stop it.'

'I did try. But I knew it couldn't be stopped, Doc.'

John stepped down from the stairs and moved everyone inside to the lounge where the fire was screaming up the chimney. Then he went over to the windows and looked out. It was near dark out there and the mist was coming down in layers, getting heavier by the minute. He cupped his hands against the glass and surveyed as much as he could, which was the lawn in front and part of the paddock over to the left. If there was anything moving he couldn't see it. He pulled the curtains and Sara stood quickly and pulled the ones on the other side of the room, looking out as she did so.

'Come back away from the windows, Sara. Everyone just sit down.'

But Doc remained standing.

'So you do have a plan then? If you knew this was coming, you must have made a plan?'

'I've got shotguns.'

Ben stared at him.

'That's your plan?'

'It's not a plan, Ben. That's just the way these things end. Do you understand? There is nothing else. Either we go out and face them or they find a way in and face us.'

There was a hiss in the corner of the room and everyone looked to see Butcher popping the cap on a cider bottle. He handed it to Pete and opened another for himself. He noticed the looks and just shrugged.

'Nerves.'

Nobody moved and nobody spoke. From outside there came not a sound save a few birds circling the trees, but then there came a commotion, like a train in the distance and people looked to the windows even though the curtains were pulled back. Then they looked at each other and finally they all looked at John who was standing near the door of the lounge which was still ajar.

G crept towards the window at the front of the house and put an ear to the curtain but didn't draw it back. There came the sound again. Like thunder. Only this was a sound made by more than the one thing. And it grew louder because it grew closer and G suddenly turned to face the group.

'Animals, John. That's animals moving.'

John pushed his way through the group and over to the window where G stood. He didn't draw the curtains either, he just a held a hand up for silence, even though there was no need because people were too scared to say a word.

'They're rounding up all the animals. They're rounding them up.'

And there was a sound of cows and there was a sound of pigs. And there was the sound of sheep too, even though the sheep had been away off on the hillside beyond the far field. And there was the sound of hens and they seemed the loudest in the disturbance and it wasn't just clucking this was squealing. And there was the sound of crows crashing through the branches of trees and the sound of two dogs, not the sound of barking but the sound of howling.

'They're rounding up all the animals. We'll have nothing left, G.'

John turned and ran his hands through his hair and G parted the curtains slightly but John stopped him and shook his head.

'We can't see out, G. Leave it.'

'What are we going to do?'

John said nothing as he pushed his way back through the group and out into the hall. There was the sound of the cabinet at the far end being opened with a key and the doors squeaking on their hinges. Something heavy was dragged out, landing on the floor with a thud.

Joey put her head on Doc's shoulder and she had her eyes covered.

'I just want to go. Jesus, how did this all happen?'

John returned with two shotguns and a box of cartridges under his arm. He threw one shotgun to G.

Pete stared at him, then turned and looked at everyone else in the room; Butcher beside him at the bar drinking cider, Ben seated at the fireplace and Lofty in his rocking chair, Terry and Sara on the couch, and Joey and Doc still standing beside the mantelpiece. Then he looked at G who was staring down the barrel of the gun and loading it up.

'G, what are you doing? We have to go. All of us.'

G shook his head.

'We can't go anywhere, Pete. We got to see this through. Sounds like the fucking pied piper is out there.'

'See what through?'

'Whatever has come down on us, Pete. We got to deal with it.'

The hall door was suddenly and violently shaken, struck by something from outside but it was not from a fist or hand or even a boot. It was more likely a log or a rock. Pete jumped.

'What the hell was that?'

John looked down the hall.

'Someone threw something at the door, Pete. Sounded like a rock.'

From outside someone called out and it was a deep voice that created a boom, penetrating the walls and the windows and filling the room. And it didn't let up. It was calling John, but by his surname.

'Casey.'

John didn't move. He just gripped the butt of the gun harder and stared at the hall door as if whoever was calling seemed to be standing directly in front of it on the lawn.

'Casey. Show yourself, Casey.'

Joey looked up from Doc's shoulder.

'Don't go out, John.'

Lofty rocked forward in his chair and joined his hands together, as they were trembling.

'They're bound to have guns too, John. Don't go out there.'

'What do you suggest I do?'

Lofty shook his head and turned to gaze at everyone gathered but no ideas were forthcoming and the only response was for the group to form a tighter circle around the fire, even Butcher and Pete left the bar and moved in close.

'Casey! Show yourself. I'm not going to harm anyone. You have my word.'

John looked down the length of the gun barrel then rested it against his shoulder, staring at the hall door. Outside the sound of the animals could be heard but instead of the discord that seemed to emanate from all over, it was now coming from just the one location, from the back, at the barn. John glanced at G who had the gun loaded and was pointing it down at the ground.

'They're out at the barn.'

G nodded.

'Sounds like it. I'll come out with you, John. Let's go. Get this over with once and for all.'

John stared at him, then at the group; it was Ben who shook his head.

'Don't do it, G. You don't have to.'

But G moved and he moved quick, despite Terry putting an arm out to try and stop him. He pulled John by the shoulder and down the hall. The clock chimed eight times just as they got to the hall door but they could see nothing through the frosted glass and besides, it was darker than hell outside.

'Casey. I see you. Open up the door.'

John pulled the bolts across, top first then the bottom, then opened the latch slowly and created a crack just big enough to peer outside onto the lawn where Heiney MacMillen stood with a shotgun against his shoulder. He was wearing a long black coat with a heavy black cap and as he spoke steam bellowed out of his mouth and nose.

'Casey. This ends here.'

'What are you planning on doing MacMillen? There's more of us than there are of you. And we've guns.'

'You've two guns. You and the lad beside you there. I've been watching you shooting crows.'

'What are you planning on doing?'

'It's done.'

'What's done?'

'Come round the back to the barn and I'll show you.'

'Why would we do that? Your brother is probably waiting there with a shotgun.'

'He's waiting there, but he's not got a gun. You'll not be harmed, no one will. You have my word, and I keep it. Not like you and your uncle.'

John pointed the rifle down at him through the crack in the door.

'You killed my uncle.'

'He killed himself.'

'You drove him to it.'

'No we didn't. He started it and it ends here.'

Heiney MacMillen turned, as he did his coat flapped like wings and he snorted steam and moved away off the lawn and out towards the barn where it sounded like every animal in the kingdom was out there kicking and scratching and gouging in the cold mud on the barnyard floor.

'Let's go John. Let's just go.'

G led the way down the steps and John followed, careful not to slip on the ice that had formed a layer on the granite. He could just make out Heiney MacMillen go through the gate and down the path. When they rounded the corner of the house their eyes began to water and it wasn't from the cold bank of mist which swirled about them. It was the pungent odour of fumes and was so overpowering that it stung their nostrils as well as their eyes and they had to cover their mouths with their sleeves as they approached. And there in the barnyard was almost every animal known to mankind which could be possibly be gathered from the one farm, and corralled they were behind the gate, each one kicking at the walls and fencing and trying to leap the gate which was shut firm and hemmed in by the brothers' tractor which had a light at the front so powerful every animal within the yard shone pale.

In front of the tractor stood Heiney MacMillen and his younger brother beside him. At their feet were several drums of fuel and in front of them the floor of the yard was wet through with it, a murky colour that flowed under the legs of the animals gathered there and was drenching the wings of the hens and even the crows which had been let loose from the traps.

Heiney MacMillen stooped and picked up a smaller container and just smiled as he emptied the contents over his brother's head. His brother —he didn't say one word. He didn't even flinch. He was smaller than Heiney and thinner too. And he wore a black coat also, only he had no cap on his head and his hair was long and greying and matted together from the fuel being poured over it. He just stood transfixed at the gate staring at John, but with a stare so full of hatred that even G could sense it even though his own eyes never even met those of the brother's. When Heiney had finished emptying the contents of the container over his brother he clenched his teeth and stooped to pick another and poured the contents of that over himself, tossed the empty into the centre of the yard where the animals were now tearing at each other in an effort to get out, and pulled a silver zippo lighter out of his pocket and held it aloft.

G suddenly cocked his rifle and aimed it dead centre at the man's chest but John held his arm out in front to stop him.

'You know what happens when you lose everything, Casey? You realise that there's always more to lose, so long as you're left standing.'

John put his gun down against the wall and took a few steps towards the barnyard, holding both hands out in front of him.

'This is no way to settle anything, MacMillen.'

'Yes it is. And the blood will be on your hands and on your conscience when you get to hell. And that's where we'll be seeing you.'

When it all went up it went up like it was going to burn a hole in the night sky. From the tiny flame of the lighter to the ground at the MacMillens' feet, a river of red and orange and blue crawled at first then spread in every direction, tentacles of flame which pulled at the legs of the animals gathered in the yard causing them to kick and bellow and snort and growl and turn in circles looking for a way out of the cauldron of heat. Skin was scorched and seared and flesh was roasted and into the sky went birds and hens, wings ablaze, cinders and embers and balls of flame kicked up in the unholy mess. And on their knees with heads bowed were the brothers MacMillen, who but for one long cry had gone silent and were being overwhelmed by the flames, their only movement being the flapping of arms as if trying to get in behind the birds and hens on the only route out which was straight up.

The shotgun kicked at G's shoulder, twice in succession, and both brothers crumpled forward as G stepped back and shielded the heat with his hand. Then the front light of the brothers' tractor popped and the tyres grew soft.

'What the hell did you do that for?'

'Jesus John, I couldn't watch them dying like that.'

John was running towards the outhouse to the tap, turning the hose on the ground next to the barn first and trying to contain the flames, for all the good it would do the animals that were still flailing about. The rest of the group had come running out of the house and they were staring in awe and wonder and horror at the scene before them, the sleeves of their sweaters and coats covering their noses and mouths, another hand shielding their eyes from the intensity of the light. G shouted at them to help gather buckets and bottles and barrels and any receptacle they could use to keep the fire from spreading and any garment or blanket to beat down the flames before the barn caught fire, then the house, then the whole Godforsaken farm.

And for several long hours they worked their way in from the circle of flame until it gradually reduced in size, stepping over the scorched carcasses of the dead animals, still warm and still smouldering and stinking so much that many were sick several times over. By the end of the long night not one animal was left standing on the farm, and all that remained was a great pile of pitch black ash and bones that were stripped of flesh, and all of it had to be carried in barrows to the river down in the woods and dumped in deep so if the water ever ran low the bones would not be revealed.

As for the bodies of the brothers, there were other concerns. Having been shot John was unwilling to take a chance of burying them anywhere or tipping them into the river to join the remains of the animals. And so late into the night the group crawled back indoors to discuss what they would do. As they entered the hall the clock chimed but nobody was counting. Time had gone up in flames, up into that hole that had been burned in the night sky and for part of that time the group sat and drank John's cider and John's poitín but nothing could banish the smell from their clothes and hair and skin. And nothing could banish the image of all that burning which had left an imprint in their minds which each and every one of them could not dispel. But they made their plan, drunk maybe, but they made it. They decided what they would do with the bodies of the brothers because nothing could remain of them. Just the thought of what they were going to do took its toll on the girls first who were taken upstairs by Doc who gave them something else on top of the alcohol to help them sleep. He offered the same pills around to everyone else and Pete took one next, then Ben, then Lofty, then Terry. As John knew there was the one further task to do before dawn broke, he declined, and so too did Butcher and G and Doc, who had volunteered to see it through alongside him.

So it was in the small hours when G, Doc, Butcher and John stepped back out into the garden. It was much colder now with a frost that cracked as they walked down to the barnyard where the bodies of the brothers had been pulled to one side and lay with skin stretched and mouths agape, two hollows for eyes gazing up at the stars now the mist had well and truly cleared.

John had blankets which he tossed over the bodies to cover them and as the others stood and observed the scene again Doc took G by the elbow.

'Don't think about it, G. Don't think about it. You hear me? You take the big guy with me.'

G walked forward and pulled up the man's wrists. They were warm and clammy just like the pig's feet the day it was burned. Doc heaved up the man's legs and they both went clumsily forward past John and Butcher, who were having a hard time trying to wrap the younger MacMillen in a blanket and lift him up as he was stiff and contorted at awkward angles.

By the time G got out into the paddock he was breathless and had to stop for a rest. Looking back over his shoulder he could make out the two figures dragging the blackened corpse, the noise was worse than the sight of it as it made a frightful scraping sound of burnt bone on gravel.

G nodded at Doc and they lifted the body once more across the paddock to the large shed used for butchering. G had grown to hate the place, its ropes and the large hooks hanging and swaying from the ceiling and the two huge tables stained from years of blood. He mostly avoided going in there. But he walked in ahead of Doc and switched on the light that hung from a chain in the centre of the ceiling and within a couple of minutes John and Butcher arrived, laughing at some joke John had made along the way. G turned on them both.

'What the fuck are you laughing at?'

Butcher threw G at glance before disappearing into the back of the shed, returning quickly with an array of hand tools and spreading them out on the table in front of him.

'Right, this one here will do for the smaller parts; ankles, wrists, arms maybe. This big mother here will be for the trunk. Needs two people basically. Now a word of advice. Once you start, don't stop. The blade will get stuck and you'll have a bastard of a time freeing it. Let's get the big one up first.'

Heiney MacMillen was lifted up as Butcher wrapped the table with large plastic sheets, scattering a few more on the ground where they stood. Each of them picked up a small saw, and Butcher a large chopping knife. G's hand shook as he stared at the man's leg he was about to carve up. As he placed the saw on the bone it bounced off it as if it were made of rubber. John was opposite him, with Butcher and Doc at an arm each. Doc eyed G and nodded at him.

'Let's just go at it.'

With that Doc bit his bottom lip and dug in to Heiney MacMillen's wrist with the saw but the sound made G retch and his mouth filled with a bitter sticky bile that was impossible to spit out. He wiped his lips and turned back to Heiney MacMillen once more, bringing the teeth of the saw down just above the knee joint and slowly rocking the handle back and forward, back and forward, trying to get a rhythm, waiting to reach the bone. He saw John looking at him out of the corner of his eye.

'Faster, G. You'll never get through it like that.'

G paused for a moment, shut his eyes, then lunged into the man's leg with the saw as fast as possible then felt it stick inside the bone, so he cut and lurched forward once more to free it, grunting and talking to himself.

Doc was finished. He stood back, sweating and flushed and threw the man's forearm into a basket. G kept cutting and cutting until the leg gave and by then he could take no more. John excused him and took him outside; he was shaking. He excused him from the other duties too, which were just as harsh and involved the scrubbing and the cleaning and working the grinder in the barn for bone meal feed, bringing everything down into fine little pieces to be spread on the far field first thing next morning.

And as night came to a close there was nothing left of those two brothers on the farm. In fact, there was nothing left of those two brothers anywhere. And G could be assured that if someone told him again they were gone, they were well and truly gone.

Twenty-nine

G woke up with a start. He could hear the sound of birds outside his window and in the distance the sound of a tractor humming, low and steady. It was warmer than it had been the last few days and for the first time there was no frost on the windows of his room.

There were girls' voices below. He looked at his watch, frowning. It was just after three o'clock in the afternoon. Then he tried counting the hours he was asleep, but he wasn't even sure when he went to sleep.

He dressed quickly and went down the stairs and he could hear Sara and Joey in the kitchen talking low. So he left by the front door and went round to the barnyard which was nothing but scorched earth. It still stank and smouldered and although they had done a good job removing the remains of the carcasses there were still parts left behind, hooves and claws and jawbones, jutting out of the ground, half buried and disfigured.

But they had saved the barn and they had saved the house, and although there was not one solitary animal left alive and it seemed even the skies had been emptied, at least no lives were lost from the group. He stood at the edge of the barnyard and he could hear the tractor over in the far field, the field that had been left to nature to do with it as she pleased all summer and all autumn when it had become a field of wild flowers and tall grass; it was a reminder of how organic a farm could be if it was not controlled by man. But the group had liked the fact that the one field was left to nature and the decision was made to leave it so. But now it was ploughed and the flowers and the tall grass were gone and John was moving up one row and down the other with a spreader hitched to the back of the tractor, and from the spreader came what looked like coarse sand.

G frowned and looked about for someone. Pete was over in the glasshouses and Lofty and Doc were in there with him, gathering the dead plants and putting them into barrows and turning over the soil. But they moved slowly, their coats still on despite it being warm in there.

'So you're up?'

G turned to see Ben, but he was looking past him and out into the field John was in, spreading the dust onto the cold earth. Ben had a yard brush in his hand but whatever he was doing he didn't seem very busy because the bristles were still clean. He laid the brush against the wall and approached G.

'G. It's over. It's over.'

But G wasn't listening, he was staring out at the winter sun taking a bite out of the horizon as it went down, staring over at John who was slowly and deliberately following the furrows he had ploughed with his tractor.

'What is it, G?'

'It's not that easy to kill a man Ben, to take away all he's got, to wipe him off the face of the earth without any choice.'

'We didn't do it, G. Do you hear me? Don't let us get into this. We didn't do it.'

John finally finished and began to slow down, gradually coming to a stop at the end of the field. He turned in his seat and looked back over the ground. With the hum of the tractor gone the farm fell back into silence.

'So quiet here today, Ben,' G murmured.

'It is.'

They both watched as John started the engine of the tractor again, raised the spreader up behind him and headed in the direction of the gate to the field.

'When John comes in, tell him I want something planted in that field. I don't care what it is.'

With that, G turned away and went back up the path towards the house, taking long strides to get there. Ben waited until he had gone then he broke into a trot to go over and meet John leaving the field. When Ben got to the gate John stopped and switched off the engine, climbing down to meet Ben.

'Was he up yet?'

Ben nodded, his hands deep inside the pockets of his overalls.

'He's fuckin' cracked, John. You better talk to him.'

John shook his head.

'Nah! G's a strong lad, he'll get through it. Has to.'

'I don't know.'

'Well what is it then?'

Ben nodded over John's shoulder.

'He wants something planted in the field.'

'Is he mad?'

'That's just what I thought. Now you better talk to him.'

John looked over at the field, the furrows slowly devoured by dusk like they were being toppled over one on top of the other. Then he spat on the ground.

'Whatever we plant in that field Ben, it'll be cursed.'

'Look, John, just close the gate and put a lock on it. We need never open it again.'

John hesitated as he looked at the gate swinging open then he pulled a padlock out of the case at the back of his tractor.

'Come back with us there, Ben, We'll go together.'

They walked back together and John secured the gate with a padlock and the chain that had been loosely draped around the bars. It was getting colder and Ben shivered as he watched John fumble with the lock a few times to make sure it was firm. The only sound now came from the huge crows that had swooped in over the field and Ben gazed up at them, their black shadowy outlines sweeping the farm in a circle before descending onto the field to caw and scrape and scratch within the furrows, tearing the soil apart.

'Do those things always fly around here after you've ploughed a field, John?'

'Yeah they do, aye.'

John put the key back in his pocket and kicked the gate one more time before turning to walk back to the tractor.

'You don't seem so sure.'

John didn't answer. He just quickened his pace.

'I said you don't seem so sure, John.'

'Haven't I lived on a farm all me life, Ben?'

Thirty

Out in a distant field a dark shadow descended on the cold damp muck. Crows, hundreds of them. They came down from the sky where they had waited, circling until the tractor had gone.

G watched them as they pecked at the ground and tore the freshly ploughed earth asunder until it seemed there could be nothing left alive in there, not even one solitary worm.

He turned to his right towards the forest, beyond a paddock, where a few glasshouses stood full of tomato plants and weeds. A river curled into the trees before dipping out of sight in the heavy growth. Beyond that, more fields, rolling into one another, up and over.

On his left, the farmhouse. In front, a fine garden that was neatly dissected by the end of a leafy laneway with a natural arch formed by branches from the trees either side. Next to him was the barnyard, moss on the concrete the colour of emerald.

A gravel path led from where he stood, up towards the front of the house, a small gate in a low wall that separated the rest of the farm from the house and gardens.

He heard the gravel crunch behind him and turned to see John heading down the path with a bottle in each hand, brown with no labels and metal hoops at the top.

'What do you think?'

'I think it's going to be perfect. Will they come back? Any of them?'

'No. They're gone, G. But all these things work in cycles. We'll start over.'

John stared out across the fields and put a hand on G's shoulder.

'It'll be perfect, G. Like you said. Don't you worry.'

G turned as he was about to go back inside and stared up at two of the largest crows he had ever seen, and he wished he'd had a gun, right there. But he knew no matter how many he shot they would keep returning again and again and again. So he walked to the front of the house, sat on the steps and looked across the lawn and down the lane to the gate and the figure of Gabriel at the top with its back turned.

'Is that end of it now, John? Tell me there are no more ghosts in this place.'

'That's it, G. I can promise you that. All we have now is our own worries, and we'll overcome them too.'

'You owe me the truth though, John. You owe me that after all I've done.'

John sat beside him and put his bottle down. It clinked on the granite step.

'Let me tell you a story, G. Once upon a time, there were two farming families. The first were brothers, and they owned a small plot of land which was hilly and rocky and not worth a whole lot as farming land. In fact, the only really good thing about that land was the view. From there you could see way across the countryside and on a clear day almost out to sea. And that farm overlooked the second, larger farm, whose lands were fertile and flat and worth a hell of a lot more.

'Naturally the two farmers didn't get on, but they had to live with each other and at times even help each other out. There was a natural spring on the top farm which formed a stream and then a river which flowed down into the lower farm. And the second farmer, he needed that water. But the first farmer, he reared sheep, and he needed the use of the second farmers' fields for grazing. So they both had agreements in place that were never actually written down any place, they were just agreements that were tacit and had been so for generations.

'Then one day a man arrived at the brothers' farm. And this man wasn't like any of the visitors that would normally appear and the brothers were suspicious at first. But this man was a smooth operator and he drove a good car and he had a firm handshake and talked well and he made an offer to buy the brothers' land at a very good price. In fact, the brothers were so astounded at the figure this man mentioned that they said they would even take half the money this man was offering. But of course, there was a catch. The man said in order for him to buy their land, he would have to have the land below too as part of the package. So he told the brothers to chew on it and that he would return in a few days for their answer.

'Then this man, he paid a visit to the farmer down below, and again he offered a very good price on condition that the brothers sold their farm too as part of a package. Now this other farmer, he was cute, he said nothing, neither hinting at whether he would take it or refuse. So the man said he would come back in a few days to discuss the farmer's answer.

'So in the meantime, the farmer and the brothers above called a meeting. And in that meeting they discussed the idea of selling the land as one package. And the second farmer, he argued that his land was by far bigger and more valuable and that therefore he should be getting three or even four times what the brothers were getting. And the brothers agreed but argued that for generations they depended on each other and one parcel of land was no use without the other. So they argued for long into the night and finally settled on a deal. The brothers would take the smaller amount offered and sell their land. And the other farmer would demand a far higher price for his land. Once the deals were made, the second farmer would then divide the money he received evenly with the brothers and they would all walk away very, very rich. And so hands were shook and nobody could be sure of whether there were ever any documents signed, but that was the deal that was made.

'And so a few weeks later the man returned to visit the brothers and this time he was more prepared and had documents for them to sign and a cheque for half the sum he had originally offered, seeing that the brothers seemed happy to leave their farm for such a small price. So they signed and they got their money, knowing that soon they would be in possession of twice that amount once the farmer below did his deal.

'So the man went down to visit the second farmer and he was prepared and had the documents ready to sign and a cheque for the sum he had offered which was much greater than what the brothers had got. Only this farmer, he reneged on the deal and he refused to sign and he refused to sell over the land. And the man was shocked and wanted to know why. And the farmer told him that you can never sell your land, your roots, and that it was worth more than any amount of money could buy. He knew that this man knew nothing about the land, about what it was good for. And he knew too this man had been buying up parcels of land up and down the country and despite his threats to return he wasn't really going to do anything.

'He knew that with the brothers off their land he no longer had to worry about them prowling around stealing as they had always done, terrorising his cattle as they had always done, blocking off the water supply and breaking dams on the river as they had always done and letting their sheep graze on his land. And effectively their land was now as good as his.

'When the brothers heard what had happened, they swore they would get their revenge. One way or another, one time or another, and either in this world or the next, they would get their revenge. And so they were evicted, their house was boarded up and their land was just left to let nature take control over it. And pretty soon, they just disappeared.

'Some people said they died. Others said they never left and have been living quietly in the house all along, skulking and hiding and biding their time. Or that they have been living wild in the forests, or out in the fields. But nobody ever found out what became of those brothers. Ever.'

G drained his bottle and went to put it down but it rolled and tumbled all the way down, breaking on the last step.

'That's the story?'

'That's it.'

ENDS

Acknowledgements

I originally wrote the first draft of this book many years ago while living in Warsaw, Poland, and like anyone who writes their first book was in a rush to get it out. But as time went on I shelved it and began working on other material. But a good friend of mine from those days, Barry Keane, said to me recently to take another look at it, because now might be the right time to resurrect those characters who I had once been so passionate about and were full of so many ideas close to my heart all those years ago. And he was right. Better to do things too early than too late.

To my loving parents and family, who I can appreciate even more now having had my own kids, thanks so much for everything.

To my agent Emma Walsh who read everything I wrote and gave me the drive to keep writing. To those over the years who gave me the chance to write, and paid me for it: Mike Hogan, Vincent Browne, Frank Coughlan and Stephen Rae. To good friends old and new, so many to mention but all so appreciated just for being good friends. And to the good people at Book Republic, thanks.